Table of Contents

Chapter 1

"Grandpa, grandpa, wake up!"

Grandpa sat there, eyes open, staring into space, not even noticing the child. His breathing was deep, regular, and very slow. That was the only indication that he was actually alive, as his huge white beard would float up and down a bit with each breath.

"Grandpa!"

The boy had been in this situation many times before, so he knew what to do next. He started slapping the old man's knees, as he bounced up and down in front of him. That caused a response. The old eyes, looking over reading glasses, began to focus on the tot jumping up and down in the small room. Then, he found his voice.

"Matthew," laughed Elu, "what are you all excited about!"

"Grandma sent me, grandpa!" Matthew exclaimed, as he climbed up on his grandfather's lap. He sat there fingering Elu's beard.

"Is it time for dinner already! Wow, the afternoon flew by!"

"No, grandpa. There is a man here to see you!"

"A man! To see me!? Well, then, we should get going, shouldn't we?"

Matthew jumped down to the floor and pulled on his grandfather's hand. Elu pretended he needed the assistance, and slowly got to his feet. Matthew kept pulling, toward the door, and the two finally emerged from the study.

"Well, nice of you two to come out!" exclaimed Mattie, Elu's wife. "Grandpa must have been in one of his trances, I bet, Matty, huh?" She said to the little boy. Matilda had fallen into Elu's annoying habit of calling both his wife and his grandson by the same name. Most people called them Matthew and Matilda, because otherwise it was confusing. Even Elu did out in company, but he savored the symmetry of the two names, even though he tended to spell them differently in his journal. So, he continued to call them Matty and Mattie at home.

The small little boy Matty was still pulling on his grandpa's finger, trying to get him completely into the other room.

"He's getting heavy, grandma," the boy exclaimed, with some effort.

"Ah, but you're getting stronger every day, aren't you Matty?" Elu observed.

"Dear, Richard is here to see you." Mattie announced.

Elu looked up, having almost forgotten why he had left his study in the first place. Then he remembered Matty telling him about a visitor. And there he was!

"Ah, LH, it is so good to see you. What brings you to our end of the tunnels?"

"Well, Bishop Eli, I thought you might need this next Sunday!" Richard called Elu, "Eli", as most of the people did. They all had some trouble saying "Elu", and it tended to slip out as "Eli". Elu responded to whichever, anyway. Richard held out a silver cross, on a large silver chain. The chain was broken, and the cross was scuffed up a bit.

"Oh, my!" Exclaimed Elu. He felt instinctively over his chest, where he usually wore his pectoral cross. He was almost never without it. As he felt where it usually hung, he recalled dropping it. The whole thing had startled him so much, he had totally forgotten about the cross and never went back for it.

"Thank you, Richard!" He didn't want to ask where it was found, since that might have required telling Mattie about his afternoon adventure, but Mattie wanted to know.

"Elu, you lost your pectoral cross! That's the special one, too, the one you got when you were ordained! It looks like it's damaged! Richard, where did you find it?"

Mattie never called Richard by his nickname, LH. She only called him Richard. The nickname thing was more for the men to do, she had always thought.

"Well, I saw Bishop drop it, coming down the stairs, but then you must have left suddenly," he said to Elu, "because it seemed like you vanished! I called your name and looked around, but couldn't find you. Of course, I recognized your cross, so I brought it right over."

"Thank you so much, LH, I really appreciate it. You're right, I will need it! So, would you like something to drink, or something to eat, or do you need to sit and rest or anything?"

Elu was pretty hospitable usually, but this time he was offering things to Richard to try to distract Matilda. She was normally even more concerned about offering hospitality than he was and so Elu figured that would get him off the hook to have to explain things. Unfortunately, it didn't seem to work because Richard had to leave.

"Sorry, Bishop, but I have to scurry home. Jennie has me on a schedule, you know! If I'm not home in time for dinner, I'm in trouble!"

As Richard left, Elu tried to simply retreat back to his study, but Mattie caught him before he could disappear.

"Ahem! Husband of mine! What's this all about? What would you be doing at the stairway? No one goes up those stairs! And how did your cross get so damaged?"

"It's not damaged, Mattie, it's just a bit scuffed. It'll be ok. This link in the chain simply came apart. It's been a bit loose for a while, I just haven't had the time to fix it. I'll go take care of it now."

"But, you haven't answered my question! Why were you at

the stairway?"

"Matilda, you know better than that! You heard LH. He came right over. He said he saw me over there just now. You know I've been in that study for at least an hour. How could I be in two places at once?"

Matilda thought about that and didn't have an answer. Elu was probably right, Richard was just mistaken. Of course, that didn't explain how the cross ended up over there, and all scuffed up, too.

Her pause gave Elu the chance he needed.

"So, if I have time before dinner, I'll go shine up the cross and fix the chain. You won't be able to tell! It's gonna be like brand new, pretty and shiny, just like my beautiful wife!"

"Hmph," said Matilda, as she watched her husband rush back to his study. She returned to the kitchen, to finish dinner. She couldn't get the whole episode out of her mind, though, and kept rolling it around in her head as she cooked.

Soon, it was dinner time. She and Elu and Matty were sitting around the table. Elu led grace as usual, and Matty waited patiently, not as usual, before he started to dig into the food. As they ate, mostly in silence, Matilda finally remembered something.

"Elu," she started, "I remember now about that loose link on your pectoral cross. I noticed it last Sunday, and I had put it in my sewing room to fix it myself! Don't you remember? In fact, I remember now, as I think about it, seeing it this afternoon, when I was in there. It was laying on my crafts table. How in the world did it end up out in the tunnel, by the stairs?"

Elu was getting worried. Matilda was starting to put things together. He realized he should never have gone out there in the first place. He just wasn't good enough at it, yet. Adeevan had warned him not to do that until he had practiced more, but he was just too anxious to try it. Now he wished he hadn't.

How in the world would he ever explain this to Matilda? He just didn't say anything at first, then he hit on what he thought would be a good story.

"Oh, I know! That young man I give spiritual direction to must have borrowed it! I remember now, he was quite impressed with it and offered to fix it himself, so I gave it to him earlier today. He must have dropped it. I'll have to speak to him about being more careful about things."

Elu was pretty proud of himself, although he did feel a bit bad about pushing the guilt off on Adeevan. It turned out, though, to not be a very good story. Matilda just looked at him with a strange face.

"What are you talking about, Elu? What young man?"

"My dear, you're getting forgetful! You know, that young man that has been coming over."

A blank look on his wife's face caused Elu to go on.

"You know! He's the one with the very dark, full head of hair, a very bushy black beard. He's short and he walks a bit funny, and even talks with a bit of an accent, that I've never been able to place, actually."

Matilda just sat there staring. It was silent in the room for a bit, other than Matty slurping his dinner.

"Elu, I haven't seen anyone that looks like that! And there was no one here today to see you before Richard came over. Are you alright?"

Now Elu was in deep. He had to think quick. It slowly dawned on him. Adeevan never was "announced" by Matilda, like Richard had been. He always just "appeared" in the study, and Elu assumed his wife had let him in. Now it was becoming clearer, and it fit with what he and Adeevan had been discussing. But, this was now a predicament. What was he going to tell Matilda!

"Oh, that's right," he exclaimed suddenly, "I always meet Adeevan at the cathedral. What was I thinking? Well, anyway, he's a very nice boy. You'd like him, Mattie. He's not actually from around here. I don't yet have his full story, so I can't say, and I'm not sure how he got into our tunnels, but he is here now and looking for some spiritual help. He even has a last name, um…Devan, I think he said it was, or…no, it was Zeman! That's it, Zeman."

"He has a last name! That's odd. I haven't heard of anyone having a last name, really, since at least my grandparents time."

That finally got Matilda off the subject for the moment, and, as soon as dinner was over, and the kitchen cleaned up, Elu darted back to his study. He fixed the chain on his pendant, and polished up the cross. Then he put it back on, and sat back in his chair, to practice his "trance" once again.

The "study" was really just a small outcropping in the old tunnel. Elu and Matilda lived in the end tunnel, one that used to be, centuries before, part of the old Chicago subway system. Having a dead-end room was a bit of a luxury down there, and the two deserved it because of their age, but also because Elu was the Bishop of Chicago. He had held that position for about two decades so far. Being bishop was how he and Matilda had come to have a last name, themselves, although it was more of a title than anything.

No one had last names in the tunnels, pretty much. Those had been lost in all the turmoil of the calamities from the 21st century. There were so few people seeking refuge there, that last names weren't really needed, then, either. Up top it was probably different, but nobody from the tunnels went up there, at least not on purpose or often, so they really didn't know.

Elu's full name was Elu Wilussit, a name that had its roots in Native American culture. Elu had, he believed, a bit of Native American heritage. When he was asked to provide an ordination name, after being elected bishop, this is what he came up with. He was prodded by his ancient grandmother, who was still alive at the time. Elu meant "full of grace" she told him. Put together, the whole name, Eluwilussit, meant "holy one" and so she thought it would be perfect for the new bishop. Matilda, as his wife, then became "Matilda Wilussit" and their grandson, when he came along many years later, they called Matthew Wilussit. They had raised him since his mother, their daughter Rachel, and her husband Tommy, had died, soon after he was born.

Chapter 2

"I almost blew it, Adeevan, I am so sorry! Matilda almost figured it out yesterday." Said Elu.

"I know," replied Adeevan, "I saw most of it."

"How could you have seen it?" asked the older man, then he thought better of the question. "Actually, Adeevan, don't tell me. I'm not sure I want to know. This whole thing is very complicated and makes my head hurt!"

Adeevan snickered, which was the closest he ever got to a real laugh. Then he got serious again: "Tell me, my friend, what were you trying to do? Remember, I told you, you are not yet ready for much."

"I know, I know, but, I must tell you, it's so heavy on my heart! I just feel that I must do something. The noises from above are getting louder, probably nearer, and more frequent. Those people are suffering up there! If I can do anything about it, I just have to! Besides, unless we do, something bad will likely happen down here, again, and more people will be hurt! You understand, I'm sure."

"Well, that's up to you. Being in a hurry has never been something I've understood."

Now it was Elu's time to laugh. "No, I suppose not, given your abilities! But, I also have to ask, have you not seen Matilda? Normally, when someone comes to my house, she answers the door, and calls me, but that never happens when you arrive. She claimed to have no knowledge of you when we were talking yesterday."

"You are a smart man, elder Elu, you surely know the answer to that."

"Yes, I guess I do. It makes sense, but this time stuff has never been easy for me."

"Oh, yes, it is! If it weren't, I wouldn't be here. I would never have found you, my friend! You have the ability. You are one of the few that does. I have found no one in this age that I can say has any such inclination. But, you have to be careful and slow and take it easy, practice it for a while, before you go trying to save the world!"

"OK, I know, I'll be more careful."

"Good, now, tell me, what exactly were you doing and how were you doing it? What do you think went wrong?"

"Well, I got into my trance here, of course. After it was pretty stable, as far as I could tell, I got up and I slowly walked around the house for a bit. That seemed to work. Matilda didn't notice anything, and neither did Matty. Then, I went out and down the tunnel. It's close to the stairs from there, and I figured I'd just see how that went. I guess I was stretching it too far. Anyway, I got to the stairs, and I looked up to the top. It's quite a ways but I just couldn't help myself, once I was there. I started up the stairs, then I decided it wasn't a good idea. But when I turned, I think I did it too fast. My cross flew up and caught on one of the broken handrails, and pulled loose. I picked it up and started back down. I think I was holding the trance pretty good but when I got to the bottom I recognized Richard. He was just standing there, and he must have been there all along, of course, but when I saw him I got startled. I think I lost my concentration just for a moment, and that's when he was able to see me. I dropped the cross, I guess, and concentrated and got back into the trance and hurried home. Sorry, I know that was a long explanation!"

"No, elder, it was very helpful. What do you think you did wrong?"

"Well, as I said, I stretched it too much. I startled myself, and then lost concentration. I guess that's all. I'm sure Richard must have been there before I started up the stairs. I just didn't see him. I was focused on that stairway."

"Are you sure he was there? If not, it may mean you lost concentration more than once or for a longer time."

"No, I'm not sure. It was the first time I had left the house and I was a bit nervous about it."

"That's probably the key thing, elder," replied Adeevan. He always called Elu "elder" but Elu was never sure exactly why. "Being nervous causes a lot of fluctuation in the trance. You need to be much more comfortable in it before you do this again."

"What would happen if I lost it again?"

"Well, that depends on what you are doing, where you are, who sees you, and all that. One thing that helps is that you live in these tunnels. The light here is terrible! People who see you may be able to be convinced that they didn't, you know."

"So, Adeevan, you have never told me, where exactly are you from? Do your people not live in tunnels? I know you're not from the surface," asked Elu warily.

"Let's just say it's a place you've never been, and never will be. In a way, it's very close, but also very, very far away."

Adeevan was very good at deflecting personal questions, which always made Elu a bit nervous, as if he were being elusive for some dangerous reason. But, Elu prided himself in being a good judge of people, and he generally was. He was sure Adeevan had nothing particularly devious about him.

"So, here's a question, I guess, a practical one. If I am successful at holding the trance for a prolonged period, but I'm doing it in this study, all alone, how can I know if I've succeeded?"

"The easiest way is to set an hourglass. You have one, I presume. As long as the sand is not moving, you are holding the trance. If the sand begins to fall, you aren't."

"Oh, well that makes sense. We have several hourglasses

around here. That would be easy."

Adeevan suggested that Elu spend the next week simply doing that, trying to get comfortable with longer periods in the trance, and maybe walking around the dwelling a bit, but not outside.

"I'll be back in about a week, at our normal time, and see how you're doing," he told Elu.

After Adeevan left, Elu tried again. In the trance, it was a bit difficult to concentrate on anything else, but it did get somewhat boring to hold it for long. Elu soon found that he could at least let his mind wander just a bit and still hold things. He kept watching the hourglass.

As he extended his ability, he began to use the trance period to go back over all that Adeevan had taught him. It was actually rather remarkable, that such a young man (at least he seemed young) had so much to teach someone so much older. Elu recalled the day they had met. It was just after Mass one morning at the cathedral. He was putting things away, when a young man knocked at the sacristy door and asked to see him. They sat and talked a while. Elu expected the fellow wanted confession, but he just wanted to talk.

Adeevan told him he was "new to the tunnels", but didn't elaborate. He was looking for someone "older and wiser" to help him with his spiritual journey. Well, Elu told him, I'm happy to help. They didn't get into much that day, but Adeevan returned a few days later and met Elu at home this time. He told Elu that he had been practicing centering meditation for many years, and had a few unusual experiences doing it. It didn't take long for their roles to reverse, and it became Adeevan teaching Elu how to enter the trance. He was still teaching him what it all entailed and what could actually be done under the trance. It was fascinating, but also a bit scary, Elu thought. He couldn't find anything actually wrong with it, but he was still a bit leery, especially when Adeevan made him promise not to disclose it to anyone else.

Because the trance seemed to allow a person to go places unobserved, and to study unexplored areas, Elu immediately thought it might be a way to get a better understanding of what was going on up on the surface these days. He had always held out hope for a return to normal, as well as a chance to honor the memory of his daughter and her husband, and wondered if he could do something about it this way.

Chapter 3

The tunnel dwellers used mostly things like hourglasses and other non-mechanical devices, since it was hard to get things repaired down there. Besides, there was very little electricity. There was some, that had been rigged up years ago with some waterwheels in the canals several levels down, but it wasn't very steady, and not very strong. They could have a few lights, and such, but that was about it. They used the lights sparingly in the tunnels and dwellings, but used them mostly for the hydroponics on the bottom level. Their main mechanism of telling time, for example, was from the huge sundial at the center of the tunnel system. That worked, but was usually hard to read, even though someone had installed a "concentrator" at the top of the huge atrium years ago. There wasn't much sunlight that came down the shafts these days, but there was enough, anyway, at least in the atrium, because of that concentrator that focused the light. Fortunately, the top of the atrium had been constructed out of aerospace-grade glass just before the evacuation to the tunnels, and so it was very strong and could withstand even the explosions on the surface.

Other than the hydroponics, not much light was needed for the "farm" down below. They mostly just raised chickens and vegetables and there was always enough to supply the families. There were only a few hundred people in the tunnels, so none of them went hungry.

Up on the surface, it was a different thing. No one from the tunnels had been up there for probably a couple generations. There was only one way up, using the stairway. It was steep and long, probably several stories high, and no one wanted to go up there, anyway. It was a dark, dangerous place. Ever since the climate disaster from the 21st century, and the subsequent race wars, the atmosphere was a bit toxic, and the dark clouds never dissipated, as far as they knew. Sunlight barely got through, and it was always quite warm and humid.

Also, as far as anyone in the tunnels knew, the race wars were still going on. They could hear explosions regularly. They would seem far away for a while, then they would come closer for a time, then recede again, but they never stopped. No one knew exactly how many people were left up there, but there must have been enough to continue fighting, anyway.

The only time the fighting had really affected the tunnel people was that day, just months after little Matty was born. An unexploded shell from the bombing up top had fallen down the stairway. No one knew how it managed to get all the way down to their level without exploding, but it did. Mass was just getting underway, and most of the people were in the cathedral, fortunately. The only ones actually out on that level were Rachel and Tommy. They were late for Mass because Matty was being colicky. They had left him with his grandmother, and were rushing to get to church, when the bomb came down the stairway. It went off before they could get out of the way. It wasn't a large bomb, so it did very little physical damage, other than killing them both instantly. Elu and Matilda had cared for little Matty since that time. Besides taking away a large part of their family, the incident only strengthened Elu's resolve to find a solution to the surface fighting.

No one, other than a few die-hard elders, however, had held out any hope any longer of ever returning to the surface, or of stopping the fighting. They used to pray about it regularly, and they once had a committee looking into ideas for re-emergence and peace-making, but that had all fallen apart about fifty years earlier. These days, the tunnel people, God-fearers, as they called themselves, were quite independent of the surface and had no reason to go back up. The surface people were so intent on fighting among themselves, that they paid no attention to the old subways and tunnels. No one was really sure if the folks up there even knew about the people in the tunnels, and everyone felt it was probably better to leave it that way.

It wasn't probably fair to call themselves "God-fearers" as if they were somehow different from the people on the surface, Elu thought. At the time of the calamities and the divisions, it was true, the very mention of God or anything spiritual was reviled and ridiculed in the greater society. It seemed that only the ones who tried to escape the violence and turmoil were religious and the ones in the tunnels certainly were. But, no one knew if the people above had possibly returned to God or not. Elu was of the opinion that they should be given the benefit of the doubt, and that they were not that different from their sisters and brothers in the tunnels, but he was in the minority. He mentioned it periodically in his sermons and homilies and other venues, but people mostly just ignored him.

Elu, of course, was one of the elders who really felt that something should be done about the situation and all the divisions, if at all possible. He thought that the first thing to be done was to get more information about what the situation was up there. That's where the trance came in. He had been doing meditation and centering contemplation for most of his life, and it had helped him deepen his spiritual life. But he had never taken it to this level, before, and this seemed remarkable. Not only could he get in a deep state, but it also seemed as if it stopped everything around him. He could stop the hourglass, just like he stopped Mattie around the house. If he could keep that going, which Adeevan said was possible, he could at least scout out the upper regions and see what the situation was. That would be the first step, and it seemed to be in reach with this new technique. Elu was actually pretty excited about it, which was why, even after almost blowing it with Richard and the cross, he was determined to keep on and see what he could do with it.

That day, when he began focusing on the hourglass, was a turning point. As he focused on the trance, and the hourglass, he continued to turn over in his mind exactly what Adeevan had said. Then, he began to think about what Adeevan had done, perhaps not said, actually. It occurred to him that he had missed a few details. One detail was the whole issue of Matilda not even knowing about Adeevan, even though the young man had been in their house quite a few times. Even at the cathedral that first day, he reflected, they had talked for what seemed like hours, but when he returned home, it was as if no time had gone by. Matilda was not at all surprised at how late he was.

For probably the first time, Elu began to realize that Adeevan had very likely cast a trance that first day and the subsequent meetings. He had possibly entered a trance, then cast the trance over Elu, and brought him into it, then they spent their time together without any loss of "time". The more Elu thought about it, the more confused he got, though. Dealing with questions of time was always difficult for him. He had read science fiction stories about time warping and time travel and he always got mixed up reading them. This seemed to be a little bit like that, and the more he thought about it, the less he wanted to think about it!

The whole idea of "casting spells" was scary, and sounded like kidnapping someone! However, the ability to bring someone along with him, hopefully willingly, could be helpful in certain situations, Elu thought. The other problem, of course, was whether this was really something evil, some devilish technique that could prove to be Elu's ruin. That's why he had been a bit reticent at first, and why he was still trying to be very careful. But, so far, he had not found any reason to not at least explore the idea. In fact, if there was such an ability out there, as the bishop he had a duty to explore it, to be able to advise his parishioners and others who might come across it. That thought seemed to alleviate any concerns and so he continued on. He had a lot of thoughts about how this could be used for good, in fact. For now, though, he figured he'd better just learn the technique for himself, and learn it better.

Just as he decided to focus a bit more, he heard Mattie calling him for supper. When he looked, the hourglass had totally drained! Well, he hadn't done a very good job of concentrating this time! He really needed more practice. Adeevan was right.

Chapter 4

"So, tell me, Matty, what did you learn today in school?" Elu asked his grandson during dinner.

"Miss Theresa took us down to see the farm!" Exclaimed the boy. "It was pretty neat! We collected eggs and petted the chickens. Then we looked at all the plants, but they were boring!"

"Haven't you been to the farm before?"

"Yes, but this time Miss Jodie was there, and she let us do more things. We would have spent more time there but the chicken house stinks!"

"Why were the plants boring?" asked Matilda.

"They don't DO nothin', grandma! They just sit there and "grow"!"

"I know," answered Matilda, trying not to laugh out loud, "but they are an important part of our food supply. We can't eat eggs and chickens all day! Besides, we don't have that many chickens! We have to keep them going, you know."

Matty was already bored with this conversation, and started to play with the "plants" on his plate, wishing there were more chickens.

"What else did you and your friends do?" asked grandpa.

"Well, coming back to school, we had races up the ramps, from the farm. I almost won!"

The levels in the tunnels were connected by ramps. There were no stairways other than the one leading to the surface. Each level in the tunnels had quite a lot of small rooms, on each side, which were used for dwellings for families, so there were a lot of families, sometimes as many as two dozen, but more often only about half that, on each level. There were about six levels, but they were duplicated on the other side of the farm, so there were really about a dozen levels. This didn't count, of course, the bottom level, which was the farm, and the top level, which was the route to the surface, but also had the cathedral on one end, the bishop's dwelling on the other, and that great sundial in the middle. It was pretty common for the kids to race up and down the ramps. Sometimes they would play organized games there, running with or kicking various kinds of balls up and down the ramps. Other times, they just ran around and wrestled. It was considered quite safe, so none of the parents got involved, unless someone got hurt. Then, Miss Jodie got involved again, because she was sort of also the tunnel physician, as well as farmer and veterinarian!

The tunnels, of course, were old subway tunnels and train tunnels, and they all led somewhere, at least they used to. Most of them had been closed up and barricaded long ago. Most of them were permanently closed, when the tunnel people first escaped down there, and they were closed off with cement and rocks and lots of debris. The lower level was still open, partially. That was where the river was. It was thought to be a tributary of the old Chicago River. It flowed along one side of the level, from one end to the other. The ramps and public area were on one side, and the river on the other, with the farm actually in-between the two. It was the widest of the levels, so there was plenty of room for the farm and the equipment.

Miss Theresa, the teacher, was really married and had her own children, but she had just always been called that. She was the only teacher currently, and she taught all the grades and subjects pretty much at once. It was tough, because of the lack of resources in the tunnels. The farm and the cathedral were really the only places to go for "field trips". She had taken the children to the sundial once, but it doesn't really "do" anything, either; it was exciting for them for probably all of about 30 seconds.

There were books to read, but a limited supply. There were

more things on the computer, but there was nothing to connect to. There was only one device, which was limited to whatever had been loaded on the thing when the calamity occurred. After so long a time, it was hard to keep it running, anyway. There were a few movies and some music on it, but Miss Theresa had used up those a long time ago, and there wasn't much else to interest them there.

She spent a lot of time on math, and reading, and "ancient" history, up to the 21st century, and they did have Bishop Eli, as they called him, come down to the school once or twice a week to "talk" religion to the younger kids. Miss Theresa taught them the basics of faith but the bishop could tell them stories, and they really liked that.

After dinner, Matty ran out to play with his friends. Elu and Matilda sat for a while at the table, just talking, not about anything specific. At least, not until Matilda brought up their discussion from earlier, again.

"So, Elu, who was it you were talking about yesterday? You had me very confused, and I've been thinking about it ever since. I don't think I've ever seen anyone that looks like you described him. What was his name, again?"

Elu winced just a bit. He had hoped she had forgotten about that. He couldn't ignore it now, or it would look suspicious.

"Adeevan, dear, Adeevan Zeman."

"Such an odd name! Where did you say he was from? And how did he get here, anyway? He's not from the surface dwellers, is he?"

"Well, it is an odd name, and he hasn't told me exactly where he is from. Actually, I had to tell him about the surface folks, he didn't seem to know much about them."

"What all do you know about this man, Elu? It sounds, I don't know, strange, even suspicious to me."

Elu felt very bad for not telling his wife about this, but he had promised not to tell about the trance and all, and if he said any more it would all come out.

"Tell you what, next time I see him, I'll introduce you, and you can see what you think for yourself. I think he's a nice young man. He's searching, just like most of us, and he seems to have an open mind about things. That's always nice, you know."

That seemed to satisfy Matilda for the moment, and Elu hoped it would stop some of the "prying". He figured eventually it would all come out, but he wanted to have better answers than he did now, when it did.

Chapter 5

Over the next several days, Elu held closely to Adeevan's advice. He practiced the trance both morning and evening, at home, in his study, with the hourglass. It seemed to be working. He was able to hold it for quite a while. At one point, he even shook the hourglass to be sure it was still working and not clogged up somehow! It was working.

It was very restful in the trance. It gave him a very peaceful feeling, and that feeling seemed to last for a long time afterward. Elu was quite well versed in the processes of discernment, and he was rather certain, now, that the trance was a good thing, although he saw how someone could become "hooked" on it and spend their life doing it. Maybe that was something that had happened to Adeevan. He was still quite a mystery, Elu thought.

Elu still celebrated daily Mass every morning in the cathedral, although there were usually only a few people there, and sometimes no one came. Later that week, he finished up and was putting things away, when it occurred to him to try the trance there, in the sacristy. He didn't actually have an hourglass, though, so he tried using a small taper in a holder. He figured if he lit the taper, and then propped it up, that would work. Normally, a taper would go out rather quickly.

This seemed to work fairly well, but Elu was not able to hold the trance for very long. He tried it a few times, then gave up. It wasn't clear to him why it was so hard in the cathedral when it was easier at home. Finally, it occurred to him that it was the unfamiliar location. He would have to practice this until he was able to hold the trance regardless of where he was, or what distractions there were around him. That would mean trying it outside of his study. Adeevan had recommended against that, at least for now, so Elu convinced himself to go back home and try.

Sure enough, back home, in his familiar study, with the hourglass, things worked a lot better. He was able to hold it for as long as he wanted. It wasn't possible to "measure" time during a trance, of course, so he couldn't try to hold it "longer", but it became easier and easier to let his mind wander some. After several days of this, he was able to even read a book, and then look up, and the hourglass had not changed.

It was towards the end of the week, that Elu decided to try again at the church. He was expecting Adeevan the next day, and so he figured it was a good test of his expanding abilities. He waited until after Mass, and after he had put everything away. Then he decided it would be nice to do this in the sanctuary, before the tabernacle. He went and, again, lit a small taper and set it on a table in front of where he was going to sit. Then he sat and tried to quiet his mind. That went easily enough. But, this time, he found he couldn't even get into a trance. Nothing seemed to work. Once or twice, he thought he had, but he was interrupted by what seemed to be a flash of blinding light! He eventually decided it was his imagination, from focusing too much on the lit taper in front of him.

Since that didn't work at all, Elu decided to go on home. He had tried for a while, apparently, because he was quite late getting back home.

"Well, you're late," Matilda said, as he walked in.

"Well," he thought to himself, "that's sure a clear indication that I wasn't able to do anything this morning. I wonder what's going on?"

"Oh, yes, you know, people like to talk!" He smiled at his wife, hoping she wouldn't ask anything further. Mattie just smiled back and went back to her sewing. Elu then went directly to the study, to try the trance again.

This time, in the study, it went very well! He found he had no difficulty with it and could hold the hourglass still for as long as he wanted. This disturbed him. Either he was not as comfortable with it as he thought, he figured, or there was something about doing it in the cathedral that was the problem. He wasn't sure he wanted to think too hard about that.

The next day, again, Elu was in the study, and there was a knock at the study door. He looked up and, sure enough, there stood Adeevan. This time Elu actually paid attention and realized the door never opened.

"Well, my friend, how is it going?"

"It is going well, Adeevan. How are you?"

"I am well, elder, thank you."

"Adeevan, one question. I never see you outside of here. I never see you when others are around now that I think of it. Where exactly are you staying?"

"You ask too many questions, old man. Instead, I have one for you: have you been doing the practicing I suggested? Have you tried anything else?"

"Well, yes, I have and that hourglass idea you had was a great one! I can now hold the hourglass without even thinking about it. I even read a book the other day, while the hourglass didn't move at all!"

"Very good progress! I knew you could do it."

"But, I do have a question, that I simply must ask. I did try one other thing. I tried to enter the trance at the cathedral. One day, in the sacristy, where we keep the supplies, I could do it but only with great difficulty. Then, yesterday, in the sanctuary, by the altar, I couldn't do it at all! What does that mean, exactly? Do I just need more practice?"

Adeevan paused, and appeared to be a bit annoyed at the question. Elu had never seen him annoyed or even pause like that. Then, when he spoke, it was with a different tone of voice.

"Bishop Elu, do not do this in a church. It will not work. That is why I tend to stay away from churches."

This startled Elu quite a bit. "Am I dealing with a demon of some sort? He thought to himself.

"Adeevan, with due respect my friend, I must know why. You know my position and my beliefs. If this is somehow contrary to the Christian faith, I must know!"

"It is not, my friend," said Adeevan, regaining a bit of his composure. "How can I explain it…well, you may be surprised to learn that I am rather well-versed in your science. Do you know what a black hole is?"

"Well, yes, it's a…well, let me see…it's a collapsed star, I think, and it's something you can't escape, because of its huge mass, I think."

"Very good. Actually, it has been called a "gravity sink". A black hole's gravity is so great, that nothing can escape it. You have been dealing with time. What you call a "trance" is not actually that. Time, as you experience it, is a flow of moments. Each moment leads to the next, correct?"

"Yes, I presume so. I don't know how else it would work."

"It's a lot more complicated than you know, but for now just go with this. So, each moment goes to the next, imperceptibly and without any delay, isn't that how you experience it?"

"Yes, of course."

"There are, if you will, spaces between those moments. They are imperceptible to anyone within the timeline itself, but they are there. What you are doing with your "trance" is inserting yourself into a gap, between time moments. It can be called "intra-time". You are "inside time" in a way. The sand in the hourglass does not fall, because the next time moment has not yet arrived. Does that make sense?"

"I'm working on it, Adeevan. I think so. So, I am able to slip in between time moments, into "intra-time", and then I can move around in the physical world, while time, in a sense, is suspended, is that it?"

"Very good! Yes!"

"What does that have to do with black holes? I'm confused about that."

"OK, let's get back to that. A black hole affects time, if you are close enough, but it is essentially a physical world event. It exists primarily in the three-dimensional physical world. It is a physical sink or a gravity sink. Are you with me so far?"

"I think so, yes."

"Well, there are also "time sinks". They affect the physical world around them some, but they exist primarily in time, not space. Because it is a time phenomenon, it takes up the gaps, if you will, between time moments. It is not possible to enter a gap if you are near a time sink."

"So where are these time sinks?"

"Only one place, that I have ever encountered them. In the tabernacle of every Christian church, behind the altar! That is why I cannot go near them. My primary existence now is within the time gaps. I am afraid, if I ever got close to a time sink, it would change my own existence! I did get close to one, once, and I was lucky to get out. It was – if you want to use the black hole analogy – it was a "white hole"! I saw a scintillating, bright white light, and I could feel it pulling me toward it. I was lucky to escape!"

"That's what I saw!" Elu exclaimed. "It was a bright light, that just flashed a few times, very briefly, while I was trying to enter the trance in the sanctuary!"

"Yes, that was it. You were very close, then! I would not advise it, elder. You may not be able to escape from it again!"

"But, I have to, every day, you know that. We have Mass daily!"

"Yes, but just do not try to enter a time gap when you are

close to it. That is the problem. If you are in intra-time when you come close to that tabernacle, you will drop out of it or, worse, be absorbed into the white hole!"

"Would it destroy me?" gasped Elu.

"No, not exactly. A black hole destroys. It is an evil menace. A white hole, however, doesn't destroy. It gives life, not death. But, it will take you from this life, and you, I'm sure, just like me, have things that you must do before you leave this existence."

This was an awful lot for Elu to absorb, and he sat there contemplating it for a while. Adeevan was silent, just waiting for him.

"So," Elu added, thinking it through as he talked, "is there anything else about time that I should know? If there is "intra-time" is there "inter-time" also? Can we move from time to time?"

Elu was actually surprised at his own question. It just sort of came out and as he thought about it, he got even more confused.

"Well, let me say, as you have asked, the answer is simply this: No, there is nothing else that you should know at this time. Perhaps later when you are ready. I think I should go now, and I'll return next week. In the meantime, you could try just a bit of traveling around your home and around the tunnels a bit while in the time gap, but do not go anywhere near those stairs, or the cathedral. Are you OK with that?"

Elu, stared ahead into space, nodding, and then when he looked over, Adeevan was already gone. Elu decided it was time for him to get out of the study for a while, and go talk to Mattie. Not that he was going to tell her any of this, of course, he just needed to talk to somebody "normal" for a while!

Chapter 6

"Oh, there you are, Elu!" exclaimed Mattie when Elu came into the kitchen. She was peeling some of the potatoes and other vegetables, getting them ready for the evening meal. There was hardly enough space in their dwelling to call them separate rooms, but on this end, anyway, were the few kitchen items and a sink.

"Yes, here I am!" replied Elu.

"You're late, aren't you?"

"Late? I've been in the study this whole time. What would I be late for?"

Matilda stopped her peeling, and turned to give Elu a funny look. Just then, it struck him.

"Oh, my, oh, no! The children! I completely forgot!"

Matilda grinned and shook her head, and went back to her work. Elu hustled out the door. It was time for his weekly visit to the school, to "talk religion" and he had totally spaced out about it. He went flying down the ramp and soon was at the school, which was just, really, one room, on the second level. As he entered the room, Miss Theresa exclaimed: "You see, children, I told you Bishop Eli would not forget us!"

Elu managed a weak smile as he got his breath and then quickly recovered.

"Of course, I didn't! I was a bit busy, but, see, I made it!"

The dozen or so kids in the class were happy to see him. They always enjoyed his stories. Elu sat on a small stool, and the children just sat on the floor, around him. Miss Theresa sat in the back.

"So, my friends, what should we talk about today?"

A hand went up. It was Darius, one of the more serious kids.

"Bishop, why didn't Jesus come to save everybody?"

Elu gave the boy a quizzical look, and Miss Theresa had to intervene.

"Bishop, we were discussing the Last Supper earlier, and Jesus' words in the Gospel of Matthew that he had come to save "the many" from their sins. They children wondered why it wasn't for everyone, and I didn't have an answer for them."

"Aha," exclaimed Elu, "now I understand. My, children, that was very astute! I'm impressed that you noticed that. Many...no pun intended," chuckled the bishop, "...but many people don't even realize it says that!"

"Well, let me see what I can do about this. Do you think Jesus was being stingy? Or was he trying to get back at some of those mean people who were after him?"

Most all of the children shook their heads. A few said "no!".

"Why not?" asked Elu.

"He asked God to forgive them," said one.

"He said even to love your enemies," said another.

"Very good, kids! You are learning so well! Jesus would be very proud of every one of you! You are exactly right! So, there are a few explanations, but, you know, this verse, and some like it, have been argued about for a long time, by a lot of very smart people. Here's what I think. First of all, you know, Jesus often used the Hebrew prophets and this phrase, "the many", was used a lot to refer to the people of God. It was sort of a jargon, you know, just an expression, and meant "all the people of God". That's us today, huh?"

More nodding occurred.

"It also meant that a lot of people would come to be part of the people of God, just like us. But, let me tell you a story."

That was more like it, the kids thought. The bishop was really settling in, now, and they were anxious to hear his story.

"There was a woman, once, who had a large family. I think there were like twelve kids! She and their father loved them all very much. The youngest one, though, was the father's favorite, because he was born when the parents were getting older, and they hadn't expected another child. Unfortunately, the older boys were jealous of that little one, and they arranged for him to be kidnapped! They told their father that he had been killed by a lion!"

"This is about Joseph and his fancy coat, isn't it?" yelled out Darius. "I know that story!"

"Ah ha, I knew I couldn't put anything past you people! You're just too smart! So, does anyone know what happened to Joseph?"

Annie raised her hand. "I think he got his coat back later, and then he saved them all!"

"Very good, Annie, although I'm not sure about the coat. Anyway, Joseph saved them, you're right, and there were a lot of them! The entire family was saved, and it was said that Joseph saved "many"! But, that's not the end of the story. Many, many years later, those twelve sons and their families had become a large nation, all dedicated to God and following him. But, after a while, they began to fight among themselves, and a lot of them were lost for good. Only a few survived. It was very sad, but do you know the reason they were lost?"

No one knew this story, so they just sat, waiting.

"Well, they were lost because they decided not to follow God anymore, but just do things on their own. They were no longer part of the "many" because they had decided not to be, anymore. There are still people like that."

"Like the people on the surface, bishop?" asked one of the kids.

"Yes, that's right, like the people on the surface. But, there's even more to the story! The people who were not lost, they started to get tired of following God, too. They began to do things their own way, and they started fighting with the people who lived around them. They got beat and became prisoners, but God was able to release them later, because they came back to him. So, even the people on the surface today could come back to God, if they chose to. They can still become part of the "many" if they want."

"Do they know that?" asked his own grandson, Matty.

"Well, another very good question," replied Elu with a deep sigh. "And, I do not know the answer! No one knows, because no one has gone up there from the tunnels, as far as I know. Maybe they do know and they have already come back to Him, at least some of them. Maybe they don't. Maybe God wants US to tell them!"

"Let's go!" said Darius. "We need to tell them!" He jumped up and started to run toward the door, but Elu was able to catch him.

"No, no! Darius, you can't do that! It's a lot more complicated! It has to be someone like me, AND it has to be something God has called us to do. For now, God wants us to pray for them, OK? Let's everybody promise me you won't go running up the stairs! And let's pray for them now, OK?"

Elu led the children in a prayer and then he left, hoping none of the kids would try to go convert the surfacers!

Chapter 7

Elu spent the rest of that day trying to avoid the whole idea of "trances" and "time gaps" and such. It was all a bit much and he felt he needed a break. He puttered around the dwelling, re-arranged the books in his study, then helped Matty with his homework after he got back from school. After dinner, all three of them played a board game, "Monopoly", that Elu had learned from his own grandfather. A lot of it was lost on little Matty. He didn't know what a house or a hotel was, let alone money, utilities, railroads, and all that. There were no such things in the tunnels, and most of it wasn't really mentioned, or hadn't been yet, in school. It was fun, anyway, just trying to figure the thing out.

The next morning, Elu was back at the cathedral. It was a weekday, and only a couple people showed up for morning Mass. After he had cleaned things up, he again had the thought of trying the trance there, instead of at home. It was tempting, but he decided against it, at least for now. He had gotten rather shaken up by his last experience, and by Adeevan's explanations.

On the way home, he had to pass by the sundial and the stairway, and he ran into Richard LH again. Then he remembered why Richard had been up by the stairs that day they had the incident with the cross. Richard was in charge of the water system. It had been rigged up many years before, probably by the first generation or so in the tunnels. Every day, Richard and his small crew would take one of the large water canisters down to the bottom level and fill it from the river. Then, they had a winch system that allowed them to ratchet the heavy canister more easily up the ramps. There were two canisters on each level, hooked up so they served the level below. That way, no power was needed since they worked by gravity. There were two smaller canisters on the top level, one on each end, to serve the bishop's dwelling and the cathedral. They had to be mounted high up by the ceiling to work, but they did a reasonable job. With so many canisters, Richard and his crew were working on a few every day, in a constant cycle of refilling them. It was a pretty good system. Of course, what Elu was recalling was that it meant Richard was up on the top level at least once every week, and so that was probably the day he saw Elu on the stairs.

"So, LH, how are things, my friend?" Elu greeted him.

"Good, bishop, good! You haven't been up the stairs lately, have you?" Richard was teasing Elu a bit, with a twinkle in his eye. But it bothered Elu, that Richard remembered the event and perhaps he had told others about it.

"No, no!" Elu laughed. "I wasn't really "up" the stairs anyway that day. I thought I had seen something and went to look, you know, but it was just a shadow! No reason to go up there, you know."

Elu felt another twinge of conscience, as he told his little lie to Richard. He was counting on Richard and Matilda never comparing notes! Richard seemed to accept the explanation and Elu continued on home.

The next few days, he continued to practice "entering intra-time" as Adeevan had called it, but always in his study with the hourglass. Sunday soon arrived, and there was the customary mid-morning Mass in the cathedral. Everyone in the tunnels came unless they were sick or something. Elu always enjoyed the singing and the fellowship, and always felt so much closer to God after the celebration. This Sunday, Matilda left right after Mass for a gathering the women were having down at the school. Elu stayed and put everything away. He then sat in the sanctuary a bit for some personal prayer, as he often did on Sunday, both before and after the service.

As he sat there, Elu had a strong inclination to enter intra-time again. He didn't want to disregard Adeevan's warning, but he also was not in the habit of hiding things from his God. After thinking about it for a while, he figured he trusted Adeevan, but he trusted God even more, so he tried it. He didn't bother with the taper this time.

Elu could feel himself slipping into the "trance" as usual. It seemed fairly routine at first. But, then, something strange happened. He saw the same flash of light he had seen that other time when he had not been able to entrance himself. It flashed briefly, then stopped. Elu figured that was going to be all, but then the light came back, brighter than he had ever seen it. It was so intense, he had to close his eyes, and he could even feel his body being pushed backward, but pulled forward at the same time. It was a very strange feeling, but it was not scary at all. It felt actually very comforting.

Then he heard it. It was not really a "voice", so much as it was a presence that "spoke" to him. Abruptly, he dropped out of intra-time, and was back simply sitting in the sanctuary, but with the voice still in his head.

God never spoke to Elu in words. But he would often get strong ideas or inclinations. This was very similar but much stronger than anything he had ever experienced before. This time, there were two very clear things that it spoke to him. First of all, Elu had a very clear feeling, a deep sense, that the intra-time "expeditions" were a good thing. The Lord seemed pleased that Elu had developed this gift, which had been planted in his soul many years before and now watered by Adeevan. Elu felt strongly that he was meant to develop it and then to use it for good, as he had been thinking about. The Lord was blessing his attempts and his desire to bring healing to the surface people.

The second message Elu received that morning was about Adeevan. He sensed a deep love and care for the man, but also a concern. The Lord, he felt, had been pursuing Elu's friend, calling him, luring him, urging him to return to his creator. What astounded Elu was the very real sense that the Lord had been pursuing Adeevan for a very long time – longer than Elu could even imagine!

As he sat there, contemplating these messages, he began to think about his new friend. Then it occurred to him, if Adeevan is a "time master" or a "time traveler" of some kind, his origins might be quite unexpected. What could this mean? Who could this man be? It was a bit more than Elu could conceive and it was even a bit frightening!

As he walked back home, Elu determined that he would work harder on practicing his new craft, but that he also would avoid asking Adeevan difficult questions, at least for now. He needed to pray and think about it a lot more first.

Chapter 8

Over the next few weeks, Elu spent a lot of time practicing his time gapping ability. He was much more peaceful about the whole thing, after his recent encounter at the cathedral. His entire reason for developing this art had been confirmed, which had a rather opposite effect. He no longer felt an urgency, or any rush, to get to the surface and "save Chicago and the world". Instead, he realized this was a spiritual gift and needed to be nourished and developed. It was a good thing he did that, too, as he found out later.

He practiced his trance at least a couple times a day. He noticed, as he got further and further along with it, that it no longer seemed to exhaust him so much. That was odd. He hadn't actually realized it at first, but it took quite a lot of effort to slip into a time gap. He was quite fatigued afterward each episode. He would often end up taking a nap, at first, but, after a while, he didn't need to do that, and he was finding he had a lot more energy at other times, too, in fact.

He became quite comfortable at wandering around the dwelling. He could focus on something outside the study and then realize that he had been able to remain in intra-time the whole while. He tried to take it slow, but eventually he began to roam around the tunnels, keeping time still until he got back to his study.

It was a good thing that he practiced, however, because he was still given to losing concentration with surprises. One day, he was down by the school, just exploring. He was admiring the various maps and other things that Miss Theresa had on the walls of the classroom, and not really paying attention to what he was doing. He turned to look at a painting on the back wall, and tripped over one of the students, who was sitting on the floor. He caught himself and automatically said: "Oh, excuse me! My mistake!"

He was startled to hear the child respond. "I'm OK bishop!"

Then Miss Theresa exclaimed: "Bishop! I was not expecting you!"

"I'm sorry, Miss Theresa, I was just wandering in the hallway and became interested in this map you have over here. I'm afraid I was being a bit absent minded! I'll see you all tomorrow, right kids?"

The kids all nodded, and Elu slipped back out to the hallway. He quickly slipped back out of time again, and stood there, resting his back against the wall, catching his breath. What a goof, he thought to himself.

After a few moments, he gathered himself and marched back up the ramp, coming up to the top floor on the cathedral side. He was still a bit flustered by the whole thing and wasn't really watching where he was going, and he ran right into Richard coming down the other way with his crew. Again, the surprise shook him out of the time gap, and the crew wondered where he had come from. Elu apologized, and then quickly walked, almost ran, back home. As he entered, the door, Matilda turned and said: "Oh, I thought you were in your study!"

Elu grinned and told her he had just run back to the cathedral for something, and went back into his study. He sat down and tried to collect himself. That whole thing did not go as he had hoped. As he reviewed the whole thing, he decided it was good practice, but he obviously needed to work on things. He didn't want people to find him in two different places at once, or to find him suddenly popping up in places like that.

The most important experience during this practice week, though, occurred the following day. Elu was once again out exploring the levels while in intra-time, and he went down to the farm. He saw several workers in among the hydroponics stands, and Miss Jodie was collecting eggs in the hen house. They were all at a standstill.

Elu wandered around the chicken yard, and was amazed to find one of the chickens in mid-air! It wasn't far off the ground, of course, but was caught by the time gap in the midst of a jump. That fascinated Elu and so he walked all around the bird, looking at it from every angle. Unfortunately, the hen had jumped very close to the river edge. As the old man walked around the chicken, he suddenly lost his footing on the bank and fell headlong into the river itself!

The river at that point was deep enough to be over Elu's head. As he plunged into the water, he struggled to stay afloat but soon found himself at the bottom. His shoes sunk into the muddy riverbed. He was stuck! He began to panic, but he had enough presence of mind to say a quick prayer. He tried and tried but the suction of the mud was too much for him to get free. He tried to stretch up and get his face out of the water, but it was too far. He began to flail around and struggle more, but, as he tried with all his strength to get free from the mud, it seemed he was getting in deeper and deeper. It was then that he began to notice something.

The current was normally rather strong because the river had been narrowed by the tunnel structures. But, now, there was no current at all. Then he realized that he did not feel breathless either. He calmed down and stopped twisting around and just stood there. He was able to just stand there for as long as he wanted to, it seemed. Then, with the panic subsided, he worked his feet more slowly and carefully, and was able to get loose and slog his way to the bank. He then worked his way out of the river.

Elu sat on the bank, pondering what he had just experienced. As he thought about it, he concluded that there was no current, clearly, because time had stopped. He also realized that, in the absence of time, he had no need to even breathe! He could spend as much time underwater as he wanted. It also then occurred to him that he had not broken the spell. He had not dropped out of the time gap, even under a rather extreme situation. That, he thought, was a very positive sign. In fact, it probably saved his life. If he had broken concentration, and dropped out of the time gap, his need to breathe would have returned, and he would have drowned! He said a prayer of thanksgiving!

The final thing that struck Elu, sitting there on the bank of the river, was that he was all wet, and his clothes were soaked and muddy! He would have to do something about that before he went back home. There was no way he could explain this away to Matilda. He had decided that it really was a good idea to not tell Matilda about all of this. It would worry her, and it might even frighten her. He washed off all the mud, as well as he could, in the river, before walking back up to his dwelling. Fortunately, he had not made any significant marks or "divots" in the riverbank for Miss Jodie or her crew to notice.

Back home, he carefully changed clothes, and ran his wet ones through the wringer. He then took them over to the cathedral and laid them out to dry in a corner of the sacristy where no one would see them. He figured he would have to get out of the time gap for them to dry, and he didn't want them found. He went back home then, much more confident in his abilities and in his understanding of how the whole intra-time idea worked.

Chapter 9

Soon, it was "Adeevan day", again, and Elu was looking forward to it. He had much to tell his friend. When they finally did get together, Adeevan was quite impressed at the bishop's adventures, especially the river event.

"That was a perfect learning situation, and a test, my friend. It was dangerous, of course, but often the best learning occurs in the midst of danger. And, as I'm sure you know, the best test is the one that could kill you! You have progressed well. You are now ready, I think, to try your surface adventure."

Elu smiled. He was anticipating that and it had been his dream for many years, of course.

"But, hear this! You are not ready to engage anyone there. There are still things you must learn first. You can explore but that is all. We need to see how that goes first."

Elu was a bit disappointed, but, he figured, this was "mission territory", and mission lands were never converted in an afternoon! Besides, the first rule of missionary activity was to learn the culture and understand the people. He had to get the "lay of the land" before anything could possibly happen.

"I understand," he told Adeevan. "But, I am still anxious to get up there. I have heard so many stories, and I have no idea if they are true. No one from the tunnels has been up there for well over two, maybe three, centuries! A lot can happen in that long a time."

"Do you even know where you're going?"

"Well, I've studied the old maps, and I have a journal that we kept from the old Archbishop, Tom Murphy. He was the one who led the people into the tunnels, and he wrote quite a lengthy account of it all. It's fascinated me since I was a child! But," Elu added, as a thought crossed his mind, "you must know all of this yourself, Adeevan, as a time traveler!"

"What makes you think I'm a time traveler, elder? I'm just a seeker, like yourself."

Elu nodded, knowing now was not the time to press his friend. That would have to come later. The two parted, and Adeevan promised to return in a week, as usual, to hear how Elu faired on his explorations of the surface.

As soon as Adeevan left, Elu was tempted to run out and up those stairs. But, he realized that he needed to be a bit more careful. It had been many years since he had studied the old maps, and read his predecessor's journal. He decided it would be prudent to review those one more time, before launching into the unknown.

The best map he had, that gave him the most details, was a rather large fold-out that showed the Chicago loop, and the areas immediately adjacent to it. It had subway and train markings, but he knew from the Archbishop's journal that not all the tunnels were marked. In fact, the one they had found back then was not on any map at all. They had been "lucky", or blessed, to have found it.

He had to lay the map out on the kitchen table to get a good look at it all.

"What are you doing with those old maps, now?" Asked Matilda.

"I'm planning," he almost lied, "to give a special history lesson to the kids at the school in a few weeks, so I need to study it."

It was only "almost" a lie because he really did plan to do that, after he had done his own in-person explorations. He hoped he would also be able to tell them about the people he had met and how he had brought them back to the Lord. Of course, that would be longer than a few weeks, but Elu figured he could always hope for the best.

After a few days of study, Elu realized he was simply going over the same things again and again. He probably couldn't be more prepared given the information he had. He was just excited but also nervous about this expedition. He decided it was simply time to at least climb the stairs. That morning, he sat in his study, said a prayer, and fell into the time gap. When he was fairly well established in intra-time, he decided it was a "go".

He left the dwelling and made the short walk to the stairway. He stood at the bottom, looking up at the sky far above. It was going to be a long climb just to get up there. He was no longer a young man. He wondered, though, if it would be like in the river. Maybe he didn't need to breathe hard climbing a stairway, either! It could go more easily than he had thought. He took the first step, then another, then another, and soon was on his way.

The climb was much easier than he had thought it would be. The stairs covered what would have been at least three levels in the tunnels. There were two platforms that divided the stairs. Each one led off to the side in each direction, but those side tunnels had been closed centuries before. As he neared the top, he could feel it becoming warmer, and more humid. The sky seemed dark, even though it was only mid-morning by the sundial below. The Archbishop's journal had described the sky as being permanently covered by dark clouds after the calamities, and it was supposedly always warm and damp, with frequent rains.

Then, he reached the top of the stairs. He found himself standing under a canopy, that had partially blocked his view of the sky. The clouds, he noticed, were not quite as dark as he had thought they would be. Of course, he had no personal experience of a "cloudy day" on the surface, so he had no idea if this was normal, or not. Everything was very still. There was no noise at all. The clouds were not moving.

Elu stepped out from under the canopy and looked

around. He was standing on a sidewalk. In front of him was a city street, and beyond that he could see a river. It must be the Chicago River, the surface portion, he thought. The river below, in the tunnels, must simply be a deeper channel of this main flow.

Then, he looked right and left. He couldn't see very far, because there were so many heaps of debris. He had seen pictures of the Chicago Loop, and there had been tall buildings everywhere. There were no more tall buildings here. All he could see were heaps of concrete and steel beams, and other stuff, all jumbled together, and nothing very tall. Everything had been demolished, it appeared.

Not sure where to go, Elu simply took a chance, and turned right. He had to work a bit at climbing some of the smaller conglomerations, and then found himself in front of a huge pile. He walked to his left a bit, came around it, and found himself staring at the most magnificent sight of his life! It was a huge body of water! He could not see across it, or find either end of it. Then he realized, this must be what they called Lake Michigan! It, too, was very still.

"Of course," Elu remembered then, "it's all very still because I'm in the time gap!"

He wondered what it would be like to drop out of the trance. What sounds would he hear? What is actually moving? What is it really like up here? But, then his caution returned, and he realized he should put that off for another trip. He walked up to the edge of the river, and looked up and down its length. He could see it entering the lake, and he also saw that there was at least one bridge that still seemed intact. It was right at the opening into the lake. It wasn't far, so he walked over to look. It seemed intact, but, again, he thought it might be better to not tempt things just yet. As he turned, he saw an ancient street sign, that was still legible. It had intersecting plates, one read "Wacker Drive" and the other said "Lake Shore Drive". He recognized those names.

As he turned away from the sign, he had a real shock. There was a young black boy, standing only about ten feet away! Elu had not seen him earlier, probably because he was hidden by a heap of trash on the corner. Elu froze. He remembered Adeevan's warning not to "engage" anyone on the surface. But, as he stared, he realized the boy wasn't moving. He almost seemed to be a statue. Elu crept closer to study him, and then saw an open place between a couple of building shells. There were other children there and one or two adults. They were all "frozen" in place. As he got closer to the child, Elu almost tripped over a small ball. Then he realized what must be happening. The children were playing a game, and the ball had escaped their playground. This boy was chasing after it. He had caught them in the middle of the whole thing.

As he looked, he realized he had not seen any other people on his walk to the lake. "Most likely," he thought, "they stay hidden in the buildings or between them. It's probably not safe to stay out in plain view around here!" Elu cautiously retraced his steps back to the street, and then decided to head back home.

Elu walked back to the stairway, along the other side of Wacker Drive, closer to the river. He had to climb over more piles of debris, and walk around some, until he found his way back. He descended the stairs, eager to re-check his maps and see exactly where he had been. It was a great first trip, he thought.

Chapter 10

All afternoon, and into the evening, Elu poured over his maps. He was able to pinpoint exactly where he had been, thanks, especially, to the street sign, but also, of course, by the river and the lake. He alternated between studying the maps, and simply sitting there entranced, remembering the lake and how huge it looked. He had read everything he could when he was younger about the lake and the city, but none of that prepared him for actually seeing it for the first time.

He thought it was amazing to see it "live" but then he remembered, he was not exactly seeing it alive, but frozen in the time gap. He yearned to see it "for real", in all its glory, and smell it, hear it, watch it move. Then, he was brought back to reality as he remembered Adeevan's caution, that the best learning came from things that could actually kill him! He resolved to be as careful as he could.

The next day, he was back up the stairs, standing under that canopy once more. He hesitated, trying to decide where to go, and decided he might as well try the other direction. He turned left, and, again, had piles and piles of debris to work through. Eventually, he found a wider street that crossed Wacker Drive. To the right, a bridge used to cross the river, but it was now mostly gone. To the left, the street seemed intact, and there was actually a path through some of the debris. He searched and finally found a street sign, lying on its back, that said "Michigan Avenue". He knew then where he was.

He walked carefully down the middle of the street, but there was not much to see except more debris, and several structures that looked like they had been skyscrapers in years past. Soon, he came to another street, but there were no signs. He turned toward the lake, and had a bit rougher going. This street was narrower and more obstructed. He climbed and walked and worked his way east, until he was once again standing just off the lake. It was still magnificent, he thought, even though it was just a formless, silent, and still blob. He walked north along what he thought was Lake Shore Drive. It started to curve to the right, and he realized it was leading him back to the bridge he had seen the day before.

As he approached the bridge, he rounded another pile of concrete and girders, and then stopped short. He could see the bridge, and it was unobstructed. He could see all the way across to the other side. But what caught his attention was a figure, standing in the middle of the bridge, looking his direction. He hadn't seen any other people out in the open like this before. He slowly came closer. The figure was facing him, with his arms outstretched, and a smile on his face. But what he was wearing was the most compelling thing.

Elu crept closer to be sure. He wanted to be careful, and maintain intra-time, and he wanted to be sure there wasn't something he was missing, being so engrossed in the man standing there. Soon, he was nearly nose-to-nose with this person. He had been right. The man was dressed in a Franciscan habit! He even had a cowl, and was wearing sandals. His face was brown, just like Elu's, and he had a bushy white beard, also like the bishop's. He had a "Tau" Franciscan cross hanging from a string around his neck. He wore a white cincture with a rosary tucked into it, and three knots at the end. This man was a Franciscan friar, Elu was certain! What in the world was HE doing here?!

As he studied the man, Elu considered how to proceed. This was just his second visit to the surface, and so he was wary of dropping out of the time gap. But how else would he find out more about this man? If he left him here, there was no assurance he would be able to find the friar again. On the other hand, he remembered Adeevan's advice, and then he remembered the times he had ignored that advice, and things didn't go that well. He decided, if I found this fellow once, surely I can find him again. Maybe, even, he is here to meet me! Elu was not sure where that thought came from, or how in the world the Franciscan would have known about him. But, the best thing was to be cautious. Elu hurried back to the stairway and back down to his study, and dug out the Archbishop's journal again. He began searching the thing for any mention of Franciscans!

Over the next few days, he read more and more, and ventured out each day. Every time he went, he saw the Franciscan in the same place, in the same pose, despite time having passed from day to day. The friar was obviously there for some important reason and kept coming back to the same place.

Elu even, one day, tried to take the man's pulse! He was clearly a flesh and blood person, not a statue. He had no pulse, but in the time gap, it was not likely he would. His eyes were clear and not clouded over. He had a few scrapes and scratches on his hands and feet, even one or two that seemed fresh and had not been there the day before. Elu was convinced the man was alive and was coming to this place every day, for some reason. The idea that the friar had been sent to meet him grew stronger each time Elu saw him.

Finally, it was the end of the week, and Elu sat in his study, eagerly waiting for Adeevan to arrive. Soon, he was there.

"My friend, do I have a tale to tell!" Elu exclaimed when Adeevan appeared.

Adeevan smiled: "You've been to the surface! I hope you followed my advice, and simply explored."

"Yes, as much as it pained me, I have to admit, that is what I did. I must tell you, I longed to hear the roar of the lake waters, to see them move! I was less interested in smelling the city, I have to admit!"

Adeevan chuckled. "Yes, you're right! That will come later, unfortunately! What was the most impressive thing you saw?"

Elu then told him about the friar.

"Adeevan, it was like he was there waiting for me! I have no idea why else he would be there, every day, the same place, the same posture, the same smile! He must go home, or to whatever he calls home, at night and then come back in the morning! He had new scratches on his hands and feet, which I bet he gets from clawing around in all that debris up there."

"Yes, he probably does. Well, what do you want to do?"

"I want to talk to him! I want to meet him! He is clearly a co-religionist, and, actually, I suppose, I am his bishop! I don't know if they kept alive the story of their archbishop fleeing to the tunnels, but obviously they kept some traditions going, or he wouldn't be dressed like that!"

"You are probably right. However, there is one more thing you need to learn before you can "meet" him. You have progressed very well in controlling the time gap, staying in intra-time, and not accidentally falling out of it. Now, you need to learn how to bring others along with you!"

This was what Elu had been wanting to hear. He knew there must be a way to do this, because it was the only explanation for how Adeevan had managed to spend so much time with him early on without Matilda even knowing about it. He was eager to learn this new facet of intra-time!

"Splendid! Show me how to do it!"

"It isn't as easy as simply showing you, elder," Adeevan replied, with a smile. "It takes time to learn."

"How much time? I don't want to lose my chance up there!"

"My friend, if the Franciscan friar has been told to meet you, he will wait. He will not tire of the wait, either."

Elu decided Adeevan must be right, and that he should leave it in the hands of the One who had given him this gift, and the mission that went with it.

"You are right, but let us begin!"

Chapter 11

"So, how do you do it? How do you bring someone along with you into a time gap, into "intra-time"?" asked Elu.

"It requires three things: control over the time gap, which you have been learning; patience, which you are still learning; and true care and concern, you might say love, for the person you are bringing along, which, I dare say, you have already."

"I have much to learn, then! Patience has never been my strong suit!"

"I know, and it is important, but not as important as the other two. Patience is needed, because it takes time and effort to learn the technique, and some people respond better to it than others."

"Is it possible for a person to resist?" asked Elu, surprised.

"Not really "resist"," replied Adeevan, "but not fully enter into it. Some people, in the gap, will be frightened and seek a way out. Their anxiety causes them to slip out of it. Others see it as an escape from reality, from responsibility, and, rarely, can become "stuck". If they are stuck with you in intra-time, you also cannot leave it. If that happens, you must not force them out, but accompany them to coax them out. It would not harm you, but forceful ejection from intra-time can damage a person's mind. You must be careful."

This information shook Elu up a bit. He was expecting to confront some difficult people, and to challenge their way of life and worldview. It could become dangerous. He shared those concerns with Adeevan.

"Yes, it could. But, you always must balance the potential good against the possible harm. Most of those who are difficult and contentious are strong-willed enough that a forceful ejection would not harm them, at least not permanently. You still have to be careful, however."

"What would happen," Elu asked, sort of thinking out loud, "if I truly cared for someone, but became angry with them during our session together. Would that cause a problem? Do I have to be thinking "good thoughts" the whole time?"

"Not necessarily, elder. If your basic approach to the person is loving and caring, that is normally enough. However, if something should happen, something say, for example, that changes your basic feelings toward them, then there could be a bad reaction."

"What kind of "bad reaction"?"

"Mostly, simply a forceful ejection from the time gap. It would, likely, however, leave a bad feeling and they would have nightmares, and be quite fearful, especially if they encountered you once more, or entered intra-time again."

"I think I understand," responded Elu. "So, how do I learn this?"

"The easiest way is to simply try it. I suggest you try with someone very easy, say your grandson, for example."

"I don't want to hurt him, Adeevan!"

"You won't hurt him. Your love for him is too strong. You could not hurt him, or Matilda or anyone in the tunnels. You love them too much."

Elu thought about that for a moment, then something occurred to him.

"Adeevan, you seem so sure about my love for my people. How do you know this? It isn't something that "shows" outwardly, you know."

"Of course, it does, elder! Besides, I have other ways of knowing."

He did it again, thought Elu. He managed to deflect my prying question! Instead of saying that, he simply asked: "Can we try this when Matthew gets home from school? He should be home soon."

"You can. You don't need me around. Have him come into the study, turn the hourglass over, enter intra-time, and then concentrate on Matthew. See what happens, and how long you can hold it."

"That's it?"

"Yes, that's it! Try this for a few days. You can try with Matilda later, also. I only suggest Matthew because he would be less likely to ask questions about discrepancies he notices. If it goes well, you can try it then with the friar. He should be easy, also. I will see you next week, elder."

Suddenly, Adeevan disappeared. Elu realized they had been together in intra-time, and it was not his doing. This must be what Adeevan does each time we get together, the bishop thought to himself. That's why Matilda never notices that I've been gone or alone in the study too long.

That afternoon, Matthew came bounding in from school. He had a whole story to tell his grandparents about what happened at school, and the farm they visited again. Matilda was busy with fixing dinner, so she told him to go tell it to his grandfather. That was the perfect setting, Elu thought, as he heard their interchange in the other room. Soon, Matthew ran into the study, all excited about watching a baby chick hatch on the farm.

As soon as Matthew showed up, Elu quietly entered intra-time. He felt quite peaceful, as he always did now, when in a time gap. He looked at the hourglass. He had just turned it over before Matty showed up. It was "frozen" with all the sand in the top, just as he wanted it. He turned his attention to Matthew, closed his eyes and imagined being alone with his grandson. He was startled when Matthew began talking again, all about the chickens.

Elu opened his eyes. Matthew was bouncing up and down, rattling on about the chickens and the eggs. A glance at the hourglass proved it was not running. They were in intra-time together! It was that easy!

"So, it was exciting, huh?" Elu asked his grandson.

"Yeah, grandpa, wow! Did you ever see a chicken hatch? We saw three of them! I didn't know chickens came in those little shells! Miss Theresa said that tomorrow she'd explain to us how they got them in there!!"

Elu smiled, and glanced again at the hourglass. It had not moved. It was working. He then listened as Matty told him all about his day at school, interspersed with descriptions of antics that Elu couldn't quite understand. At any rate, he knew that it usually took his grandson at least fifteen minutes after school to calm down and decide to play with his toys or something. He waited, and eventually Matty was done. Elu caught him before he was about to leave the study.

"Matty, look, my hourglass. It isn't working!"

Matthew looked at the hourglass. It wasn't running. The sand was stuck in the top. But, always preferring things that moved, this didn't seem to impress the little one. He just said: "Oh, it must be stuck, grandpa."

Elu reached over and pretended to shake the thing, and he released his hold on intra-time at the same moment. Just then, the sand began to flow again, and Matty exclaimed: "See, grandpa, I told you so!" Then he ran out of the room to find his favorite toys. He knew it wouldn't be long before grandma would make him work on homework, and he had playing that needed to be done, first.

Elu sat there, pleased with the whole process. Not only had he been able to hold the time gap, but he was also able to bring Matty rather easily into it, and he was able to convince himself that Matty could be easily released from it, as if nothing had happened. He was ready to practice on Matilda, now!

Chapter 12

Elu felt he needed to work more on patience, so he decided it would be a good idea to only practice the new skill once a day. He tried to spend the rest of the time praying about it, and contemplating it, trying to learn from what he had experienced. That evening after the first experiment with Matty, he began to turn the whole thing over in his mind. He realized there were several things that Adeevan had not clarified. He began to list the questions in his head.

First thing that he wondered about was whether or not he needed to actually know the person he was trying to bring into the time gap. That had not occurred to him at first. Of course, he had never met anyone he didn't really know, until he came across the Franciscan on the bridge.

Second thing was, how close did he have to be to bring someone into intra-time with him. If he walked too far away from someone who was with him, would they drop out of the time gap? Would that be like forcing them out of intra-time and would it be a bit brutal?

A third thing he thought of was how many people could he bring into a gap at once. Adeevan had never answered any of these questions. It was mostly up to Elu to figure these out, he assumed. In fact, it might be different for different people, and it might depend on who was doing it, how strong their gift was. As he thought it through, Elu realized there was a lot more to learn about all of this.

His experience with Matty seemed to indicate that the individual with him wouldn't notice any weird time breaks and would likely remember everything that went on, but, again, he wondered, would that always be the case?

Later that same day, Elu decided to see if he could bring Matilda into the time gap with him. He sat in the study, and stabilized himself in intra-time. Then he got up, and walked out to the main room, where she was sitting. She was working on some sewing, and, of course, was "frozen". He sat down next to her on their small sofa. He reached over and upturned the smaller hourglass that was sitting on the table in front of them. It was now full at the top, and not moving, of course. He then concentrated on bringing his wife along with him. Suddenly, she began sewing, and humming. She had been humming a tune from church, Elu had noticed, before he dropped into the time gap in the study. It stopped when he had entered intra-time. Now, it began again.

He looked over and saw her hands moving. Then he looked at the hourglass. It was still not moving.

Just then, Matilda shook with a start.

"Elu! What are you doing here? I didn't even see you come in!"

"You were very intent on something, either the sewing or your humming, I guess!" He declared.

Matilda looked at him with wide eyes, not sure whether to believe him or not, but not sure what else to think, anyway.

"I guess I must have been! I didn't think I was, but…oh, my! Look at that hourglass, it's not working. It must be plugged up."

Elu intercepted her arm before she could turn the thing over. He didn't want her to discover what was going on, exactly.

"Oh, yeah, I had the same problem with mine in the study. I have to take it to the workshop. These things get stuck sometimes, you know. So, tell me, what was the tune you were humming? I recognize it but I couldn't place it."

As Matilda told him about the hymn, he eased them both out of the time gap.

"Oh, Elu, look, the hourglass is working again! That is so strange!"

He looked and, sure enough, the sand was dropping. That made sense. Now he wanted to see if he could seamlessly move back and forth. With very little effort, he simply concentrated on it and the thing stopped.

"Well, now it's stopped again! Elu, you do need to fix this thing. Something must have gotten in there, although I don't know how in the world it could have."

Elu decided the best thing to do was to simply exit intra-time and not give Matilda any more reason to question things. It seemed that things were working as he wanted them to. He ended the session and took the hourglass into the study, promising to work on it. Matilda went back to sewing and humming.

Over the next few days, Elu tried out his new ability with several others in the tunnels. He tried it on the farm with Miss Jodie, he tried it on one of the levels with Richard LH, and then he went to the school. In the classroom, he discovered, he could bring the entire classroom with him into intra-time, but it was a bit harder to maintain it for long. Still, with practice, he figured it would work. He now felt ready to meet the friar on the bridge.

Chapter 13

The very next day, Elu made his way up the stairway. He had entered intra-time in his study, and then left. Before he went, he made sure to be presentable. He reasoned that the man he had seen on the bridge must be a Franciscan friar, a religious man. He also figured he would recognize someone in clerical clothing, so Elu dressed in his crispest Roman collared shirt, and hung his pectoral cross around his neck. He didn't want to frighten the man, but he did want it to be understood where he was coming from and what type of person he was.

The surface hadn't changed in the days since his last visit. He knew better where he was and how to get where he wanted to go. He walked resolutely east on Wacker Drive until he rounded the piles of debris at the intersection with Lake Shore Drive. There was the bridge again. He tried not to look at the bridge until he was ready. Then, sure enough, there was the Franciscan again, in the same posture.

Elu stopped and considered the situation. He decided that abruptly appearing nose-to-nose with the man would probably scare him to death. He still didn't know how far out he would be able to reach anyone to bring them with him into the time gap, but all he could do was try. He stood at the foot of the bridge, figuring he was at least 50 feet away from the fellow. He concentrated and felt something change. As he gazed ahead, he thought he could now see the man wavering some.

Elu took a deep breath, and began to walk slowly toward the religious in the middle of the bridge. As he came closer, he called out: "Dominus vobiscum!" He was amazed when the friar suddenly dropped to his knees, and exclaimed: "Et cum spiritu tuo!" The man's grin widened, and he shouted out: "My father! My bishop! I knew you would come!" He stretched out his hands to Elu, as he drew closer.

"My friend, I am Bishop Elu, who are you, friar?"

"Your excellency, I am Brother Leo, Leo Mizzl, your servant!"

"Brother Leo, how long have you been waiting here?"

"It has been several weeks, your excellency. The Spirit told me you would come. I was told to wait on this bridge, to wait patiently. I was told I would meet the bishop, and that when I met him, suddenly the roar of the lake, the wind, all the turmoil of the city, would suddenly cease. It has! It is now quiet. I trust the Spirit. I knew you would come, Bishop Elu. Please, bless your servant!"

Elu gave Leo his blessing and then told him to stand up. Elu was uncomfortable with the friar kneeling before him. Besides, as an old man, it was awkward trying to lean over to talk to him.

"Brother Leo, what congregation are you from? Are there many others?"

"Alas, bishop, I'm the last one. My congregation was the Franciscans of Streeterville. We were formed by Archbishop Tom Murphy, just before the calamity. He left us in charge of Holy Name Cathedral when he left to find help for the people."

"Yes, the Archbishop was my predecessor. We dropped the "arch" before the title several years ago."

"Where are you now, bishop?"

"Brother Leo, I've been asked by the Spirit to be very cautious about certain information. Our position is, or may be, still tenuous. I hope you understand."

"Of course, your excellency!"

"In fact, Leo, we should get off this bridge, and go somewhere we can talk."

"Oh, yes, bishop. I'll lead you back to our priory. It's a bit of a walk if that's OK with you."

"That's fine, my friend. We're safe for now, anyway."

Leo then led Elu north on Lake Shore Drive, past Navy Pier, and then several blocks to a relatively wide cross street. Elu counted the blocks, and searched his memory, trying to figure out where they were and where they were going. Leo turned west on that wider street and Elu found a street sign. It said this was Chicago Avenue. After a bit of a longer walk, around more piles of debris, they came to a corner and Leo stated they had arrived.

The intersection didn't look much different than any other. The streets farther from the lake were more clogged with junk and concrete blocks, and other things, than closer in. It was hard to catch any landmarks, even for someone familiar with the place. Elu knew it only from Archbishop Murphy's journal and some pictures, and, of course, his maps.

"Where, exactly, are we, Leo?"

"Bishop, this is our friary, in the lower level of this building."

All Elu could see was another pile of rubble. He wasn't sure exactly where the "building" was that Leo meant. Then, he saw a stairway, going down only about ten feet, to a door. There was really just a doorway. It looked as if there hadn't really been a door there for a long time.

He followed Leo down the stairs and in the door. It was a bit dark, but Leo had a torch burning. As they entered, Elu caught sight of a sign, very dirty and smeared. He gazed at it for a moment, then rubbed it clean with his sleeve. The sign said: "Holy Name Cathedral, Lower Level."

Elu stood there gazing at that sign for a long moment. He felt tears coming and blew his nose. He wiped his eyes, and said to Leo: "This is our old cathedral, Leo! It has been totally destroyed!"

"Yes, bishop, just like almost every other building in the

city. It's sad, but it was done many years ago. Now is a new day, and the Spirit is starting to move!"

Elu smiled and nodded, and followed Leo inside, where they sat and began to talk. Leo even was able to provide Elu a cup of very weak coffee, for which the bishop was very grateful.

On the wall above them was the torch that Leo used for light. Elu noticed that the flame appeared "frozen". It was not acting like a normal flame. He hoped Leo wouldn't notice.

Chapter 14

"So, bishop, the Spirit told me you were coming and to go welcome you, but never told me why you are here."

"It's a bit of a long story, my friend, but the bottom line is that I have had a burning desire, all my life, to do something about the constant fighting up here. We can hear it from where we live. The Lord has finally given me reason to believe that now is the time. Of course, I have no idea what the situation is on the surface. This is only the second or third time I have been above ground. I'm doing "reconnaissance", you might say."

Just then, Elu realized he had given away a clue to the tunnels, as he talked. He hoped Leo wouldn't notice that, either, although he was pretty sure the friar was harmless. He figured it would be best to just continue the discussion as he had started it, talking about "up here" and "down there".

"Ah, a wise thing to do, excellency!"

"Yes, and I suspect it starts with you! What can you tell me, in general terms, of course, about what's going on up here?"

"Well, I suppose I should start at the beginning. You know about the archbishop leaving. He led a small group of families to take shelter away from the war. It was a mixed race of people, as I have been told, but perhaps you know this part better than I do."

"Yes," Elu replied, "we were told that our ancestors were a mixed race of people, African heritage, European, Native American, Asian…pretty much the entire spectrum. They intermarried over the centuries, and so, as you can see in my own face, I am a mixture of them all!"

"As am I, bishop," the friar said, with a gleam in his eye. "As you can see, you and I are very much alike!"

"Age-wise, too, I would venture to say!"

"Yes, I think you're right about that!"

"So, Leo, who all was left up here?"

"Well, the fighting and the environmental collapse left very few people even before the archbishop's contingent left. The population was sparse to start with and it has declined ever since. I am told, although I have no direct evidence, that the same thing happened all over the country, in fact all over the world! The world population is likely to be very small today. I have been told, again, that it is hard to find anyone living elsewhere in North America. The coasts are under water for many hundreds of miles, of course."

"So sad, it's almost like Noah's flood, isn't it?"

"Yes, excellency, in fact I have heard it compared to that."

"How about your own order? You said you are the last of the Franciscans here?"

"I am, bishop. There were never very many of us. Archbishop Murphy left us here to guard the churches, and he left a few priests to assist us, to allow us to have the sacraments. I don't think he believed they would be gone for long. No one understood the severity of what was going on at that time, you know."

"Of course not. I understand that," replied Elu.

"Well, over time, we lost the priests, of course. There were a few families that didn't follow the archbishop, and they all pretty much huddled around the cathedral, here. My own family was one of the last of them but even our family died out after a long while. When I was of age, I naturally joined the order. Soon after that, my parents died and then soon after that my Franciscan brothers followed. I have been alone here, now, for about twenty years."

"Oh, my, Leo, I'm so sorry to hear that! You have had no fellowship at all?"

"No, bishop, other than I occasionally have been able to interact with some of the women and children in the two warring communities, the "Brigade" and the "Brotherhood", as they call themselves. Not often, though, and only with some trepidation on their part. I must tell you, excellency, they are all tired of this war of theirs! There are certain hard-liners who will not let it go, though."

"I see. How many of them are there, do you think?"

"Well, that's hard to determine. On the north side, here, is the "White Power Brigade". Their territory is basically north of the river, and between Michigan Avenue and the lake. They pretty much stay south of Chicago Avenue, too. On the south side, south of the river, is the "Black Brotherhood". They also are mostly between Michigan Avenue and the lake, and not very much farther south. I would estimate each group has only about 25-30 adults, plus a few children. They have kept themselves "racially pure", so they look nothing like us, of course," Leo chuckled a bit.

"And they continue to fight one another? I assume that's what we are hearing. We hear explosions nearly every day, some closer, some more distant."

"Yes, Father, that's it. I'm not sure they are killing anyone these days. Their numbers don't seem to change much, as far as I can tell. I think they are mostly waging war on the old buildings and other structures around the city!"

"Do you know their leaders? Are they approachable?"

"That might be stretching it a bit. I know their wives. It might be possible to approach the leaders through their families."

"Excellent idea, Leo. Do you think you could set up a meeting for me?"

"I probably could, excellency. Probably only the wives to start with and probably only one side at a time, but I could see about it. Where would you meet them?"

"Where is a good place, Leo? Where would they feel less vulnerable? Would this place work?"

"I think it would, bishop. In fact, if we met here, I might be able to get the two wives together. I will have to see about that."

"Leo, this is a great help. I need to pray about all of this for a bit. And, I'm wondering, would you want to come with me to our tunnels? I hate to see you living in the middle of a pile of rubble!"

Mentioning "tunnels" did not seem to startle the friar. Elu did that on purpose, to see his reaction. After all, he had more or less given it away, anyway.

"Bishop, thank you, but I'm an old man. I've lived here all my life. I am fine here."

"Well, OK, then. When should we plan to meet again?"

"Give me a week, bishop. If you could meet me here exactly one week from today, I will try to have those folks here to greet you."

"I will do that, Leo, and, thank you so much!"

Elu rose, and Leo again asked for his blessing. After the blessing, Elu turned, and, as he walked up the stairs, he released Leo from the time gap. He turned to see, and Leo was again frozen in time. Elu didn't leave the time gap himself until he was safe again in his study back home.

Chapter 15

Over the next few days, Elu spent a lot of time in meditation and prayer, seeking the Lord's will and asking what he should do. One day, after daily Mass, he decided to attempt once again to enter intra-time in the sanctuary, right under the tabernacle. He had avoided that since the last time, not for any particular purpose, but he was just pre-occupied.

Just as the last time, he sat before the tabernacle and closed his eyes. He gradually dropped into the time gap, and again, there was the almost blinding light.

"Lord, are you there?" Elu asked the light.

"Yes, Elu, I am here," came the reply. It was so clear, it startled the bishop. He recovered quickly, though, and went on with his question.

"What should I do about the surface people?"

Instead of a direct answer, which Elu didn't really expect, he heard the Voice tell him: "Elu, open your eyes."

That seemed a bit strange, and Elu wondered if it was meant literally or if it was some kind of metaphor. He decided it couldn't hurt. He had always had the habit of praying in the sanctuary with his eyes closed, and so this time he opened his eyes.

Immediately, he felt a cold wind. The sanctuary and its lights were gone. There was a cloudy sky overhead, and, as his eyes got used to the scene, he realized he was kneeling on a hill. He looked around and saw a small group of people, dressed in flowing robes. Beyond them, he could see what appeared to be a tall stone wall in the distance. Even though he was certain he was in the time gap, and the people were not moving, there was a chilly wind hitting his face, and the clouds above seemed to roil menacingly. Then he heard the Voice again.

"Look this way, Elu."

The voice came from just to his right. It seemed to be above him. He turned his head that way and saw a thick wooden plank, that seemed to be stuck in the ground. It grabbed his attention. It was rough and slightly bent, but sturdy. A man was standing by it, and he was dressed very differently. In fact, he looked like the pictures Elu had seen of Roman soldiers.

"Up here, Elu, I'm up here," came the Voice again.

Elu raised his eyes, and the sight astounded him. He almost fainted. He found himself staring directly into the eyes of a man who was attached to the top of the plank, hard up against a cross bar that was attached higher up. He looked terrible! His face was all bloody, and he had the smallest of cloths covering his mid-section. But, in spite all of that, he was giving Elu a glorious smile!

"I am glad you are here, Elu. I have much for you to do!"

"Lord, where are we? What is this?" Elu knew, without being told, who the man on the cross was!

"Your friend Adeevan explained it to you. You are in what he called the "time sink" of the crucifixion, Elu."

"Why are you still on the cross, Lord?" Elu blurted out.

"Elu, my friend, I will be on this cross until the end of time. I have been on this cross since the closure of Eden. My crucifixion broke through into space-time in Jerusalem around the year you know as 33 AD, but it has existed since the beginning and will until the end. The tabernacle is the connection. The Eucharist connects all of space-time to this event. That is why Adeevan called it a time sink, although he doesn't fully understand it himself."

"And neither do I, Lord!" Elu cried out. "I thought you were in heaven, at the right hand of the Father!"

"Of course, I am, Elu. But that is beyond time. It has to do with eternity and is beyond your understanding at this point."

"What can I do?" Elu asked.

"See my wounds. See my love and my total outpouring for all people. That is what you must do. You must become "me" to those people on the surface! That is how you will save them, Elu."

"I understand," Elu stammered, although he really had no clue. The man on the cross, of course, understood that, and simply smiled at him.

"You will, Elu, you will. Now, return to your own time."

As the Lord said those words, suddenly Elu felt himself almost forcefully expelled from intra-time. He was once again in his own cathedral, sitting in his own sanctuary. The chill he had felt was gone. The candles were still burning, and now they were dancing like normal flames. Elu slowly rose from his chair, and stumbled home.

Chapter 16

Elu was sitting in his chair in his study, motionless. He felt numb and peaceful all at once. Suddenly a figure appeared before him.

"My friend, you appear perplexed." It was Adeevan.

Elu shook himself into consciousness and focused on the man in front of him.

"Adeevan? Is today our day to meet?"

"No, elder, it is not. But, I felt a tremendous pull in the time stream, and realized something must have happened. I am here to investigate, as you might put it."

"Yes, yes…something tremendous did happen," Elu said, slowly, as he gathered his thoughts. "Something tremendous, indeed!"

"Have you been in the sanctuary, elder?"

"Yes! Yes, I have been. Adeevan, it was nothing like what you said it would be. I "survived", even though you told me I wouldn't."

"Do you resent me for telling you that?"

"No, actually, but I wonder if you misled me on purpose or if you simply told me what your own understanding was."

"You're right about that. I told you what I believed to be true. Apparently, either I was incorrect, or something else happened."

"Adeevan, tell me, why do you avoid Him?"

For the first time ever, since Elu had met the time traveler, Adeevan seemed to not have an answer. He was speechless. He turned his face away from Elu and took several deep breaths.

"Elder, I don't know what you mean."

Elu simply responded, very gently, "Yes you do, Adeevan. But, let it be for now. You'll tell me when it's time. Now, I have a decision to make, and you may be able to help me."

"I will do what I can, elder." Adeevan turned back now to face the bishop, and seemed to re-engage the conversation.

"I have been to the surface. I have met a man up there, who knows who I am. He was left there with companions, to guard the old cathedral, by my predecessor. He is now alone, and he wants to assist me in my mission."

"This is the friar you saw on the bridge?" asked Adeevan.

"It is. He recognized me as his bishop as soon as he saw me."

"What decision do you have to make?"

"At least two, rather immediately. I feel I must tell Matilda what I'm doing, and I see no way to do that without giving her some idea of the time dilation. Also, Brother Leo, my Franciscan friend, is going to set up a meeting next week with some of the surface people. I need to decide exactly how to conduct that meeting, what to say and do, and whether to do it in the time gap."

"Well," said Adeevan, "it is up to you, elder. I would guard against the surface people knowing anything about intra-time, and I wouldn't be quick to even tell your wife about it. It's hard to predict how someone would react to this knowledge."

"Of course, but, I'm not comfortable keeping secrets from my own wife. I'm sure you understand that, Adeevan. You have a wife, I believe – or at least had one."

"Yes, I did, and do, and I get it. It's up to you."

"One other thing, my friend. It was so painful to see the destruction on the surface. It especially hit me to see our old cathedral in such ruins. Virtually nothing was identifiable. The thought occurred to me, what if we could go back in time and prevent all of this. With your experience, you could likely do that, could you not?"

Adeevan paused again, searching for the right words.

"What you ask is neither easy nor prudent! Many things would change. Besides, I am not sure it would be possible."

"But, you could go back in time? It is possible?"

"Elder, we have been dealing with intra-time. There is another feature of time, called "inter-time". In inter-time, a person who is already in an intra-time gap can access another, adjacent intra-time gap, and jump from one part of the time stream to another. There are multiple problems with this, however. First of all, it is very difficult. Secondly, there is no way to know where in the time stream you are jumping to. But the worst problem is that there is no way to know WHICH time stream you are entering when you do that."

"WHICH time stream?? What do you mean, which?"

"This is a bit beyond normal comprehension, but you should just know, there are multiple time streams. In fact, there are actually eight of them. They all came into existence at the same time, leading from the same place. They all converge on the same place. But, in between, they intertwine. It's like – if you forgive the humble analogy – it's like a bowl of spaghetti! Time streams lie adjacent to one another, but they are so tangled, you wouldn't know which one you are entering."

This was a bit much for Elu. He sat there for several minutes, before replying.

"Are you saying there are eight different copies of this world? Eight different "me's"!?"

Adeevan chuckled. "Not at all, elder! There are eight time streams, but human beings are only in one of them. However, if you enter one, you may not be able to get back to this one, and certainly it would be very hard to get back to the same time you left!"

By now, Elu's head was reeling. He couldn't even remember the original questions he had asked Adeevan. It was all a bit much.

"I must go, elder. But, before I do, a bit of advice. Do not meet the surface people without the protection of the time gap. If something bad happens, you can simply exclude them from intra-time, and that freezes them, you know. Just be very careful."

Elu nodded, as Adeevan simply faded from view. It was time to make some decisions.

Chapter 17

"Matilda, we need to talk about something," Elu said, as he came out from his study.

Matilda was sitting on the couch, reading, and looked up when he came into the room.

"OK, what about?"

"I need to tell you about some things I have been doing. But, first, let me show you something."

He reached over and turned over the large hourglass sitting on their coffee table. It began to drain, as usual.

"Are you timing our talk?" Asked Matilda teasingly.

"No, dear, but watch this."

Elu then slipped into intra-time, bringing Matilda with him.

"Oh, this thing is stopped up again!" Matilda reached over and shook the hourglass. Nothing happened. She shook it a few more times, and still nothing.

"That's strange! What's wrong with this thing?"

"Mattie, watch," said Elu, as he pointed to the hourglass. He slipped them both in and out of intra-time a few times, and the sand stopped and started each time.

"Elu, what is going on? I have a very strange feeling about this!"

Just then, Matthew bounded into the dwelling, back from school.

"Hi, grandma, hi, grandpa," he yelled.

Suddenly, he was quiet. Matilda had only glanced at him when he came in. Her attention was on the hourglass. But, when her grandson became so uncharacteristically silent, she looked up. There was Matthew, suspended in midair, not jumping, not falling. His mouth was open and he was looking right at her, but there was no sound.

Matilda hesitated for a moment or two, then exclaimed: "Matthew!? Elu, what is happening?!"

Elu patted her hand, and said: "Nothing bad, Mattie, not at all."

"Why isn't he moving? Oh, my, Elu, what's wrong with him?"

Just then, Matthew landed on the floor, and started up his banter again.

"It was fun in school today. Did you know…" and he stopped in mid-sentence. Again, he seemed to be frozen. Matilda looked at him and then back at Elu.

"Matilda, my dear, you are not going crazy, although I know that's what you think. This is part of what I need to tell you. The Lord has given me a special new gift, the gift of stopping time. I have simply stopped Matthew in the middle of what he was doing, and I have brought you along with me to observe it."

This was a bit much for Matilda. She had no idea what Elu was talking about, but whatever it was scared her to death! She was so scared and anxious about it that Elu could see her flickering. She acted almost like one of those old-time movies that Elu had seen as a boy. The images would flicker, and stop and start. He realized that it was her fear that was causing her to not be stable in the intra-time trance. As he held her hand and talked softly to her, she began to stabilize. "Please, Matilda, don't be scared. This is a special gift the Lord has given me. He gave it for a special purpose, and that is what we need to talk about. Now, I'll release Matthew and let him get on with his homework."

"…that chickens can't fly! All birds can fly, but not chickens!!" exclaimed Matthew. Then, he ran into his little niche and started to get out some toys.

"Matthew," called Elu, "do you have homework to do?"

"Yeah, not much. I'll do it, just in a minute."

Matilda was sitting there with her chin practically on her chest and her eyes wide, glancing back and forth from Matthew to Elu.

"Mattie, I didn't want to scare you, but you needed to see that. Please, say something!"

"Elu, I don't know what to say. I have never seen anything like that before! Please, tell me it isn't true! Please tell me that my husband is not some kind of magician or witch or something!"

"Mattie, let us pray about it," Elu suggested. The two of them sat holding hands on the couch for a while. As they prayed, Elu could feel a certain warmth descend on them, and when he looked up, Matilda was smiling at him.

"Now, I get it! You're right. I don't know what scared me so, but I see now. As we began the prayer, I felt a warmth and then I just…understood! But, you're right, we need to talk! What are these plans of yours? How are you going to use this "gift"?"

Elu was amazed, and relieved.

"You certainly came around quickly!"

"It was the Lord. He spoke to me while we were praying. But, Elu, don't expect everyone to react this way. I had a sense from Him that you have a serious mission, and it may involve people who won't be in tune to the Spirit as much as we are. You have to be careful. Remember…how we lost Rachel and Tommy! Those people are dangerous up there!"

"I know, dear, but even they deserve our love and forgiveness, and they need the Lord! You know that!"

Mattie nodded, with tears in her eyes. They spent the rest of that evening discussing the plans for the surface people, and what exactly needed to be done. Matilda would become Elu's "prayer partner" for this adventure. She only had one request: "Please, Elu, bring Brother Leo home so I can meet him! I know he is comfortable in his little friary, but perhaps he needs a bit of a push to enter our community!"

Elu promised to do what he could.

Chapter 18

A week after his first visit to the friary, Elu was on his way there again, for the promised meeting with Brother Leo and, he hoped, the wives of the faction leaders. He had spent the last few days in prayer and discussions with Matilda, deciding exactly how to approach the situation. They finally decided it would be best to just see what common ground there might be and explore their thoughts on ending the fighting.

Elu entered intra-time before he left the tunnels, and then decided to try exploring further west along the river. He found a bridge that was still intact, and a street sign called it State Street. He remembered from his map studies that it should take him straight north to the old cathedral. Of course, nothing in Chicago was straight anymore. Elu had to detour around huge piles of debris and trash. But this route was still faster than going all the way to the lake and over that other bridge.

Soon he was at the old cathedral, and found himself standing at the top of the friary steps. He descended and found Brother Leo and two women, sitting, and waiting. They were "frozen in time" of course. Brother Leo was sitting between the women, who were sitting about as far apart from one another as possible in the little room. They were not looking at one another, and, even without motion, Elu could tell from their postures that they were not exactly happy about being in each other's presence.

Elu stepped back out and up the stairs, in order to bring those three into the time gap with him. He didn't want to introduce another complication by simply appearing out of nowhere. Then, when they were safely enfolded into the gap, Elu rapped on the broken-down wooden gate. He called out: "Brother Leo, are you there? It's Bishop Elu. May I come in, please?"

Brother Leo called back: "Yes, please, bishop, your excellency, come in! We've been waiting for you."

Elu descended the stairs again, and entered the space. He smiled at them and said: "Thank you, Brother Leo. Ladies, it is an honor to meet you. I apologize if I'm late!"

"Oh, no, bishop! You are right on time. Our guests have just arrived, in fact. May I get you some coffee, excellency?"

"Thank you, Leo, that would be very nice."

Elu was pleased to see the women didn't "flicker" like Matilda had. They seemed to be quite stable in the time gap. He went to each of the women in turn, to offer a handshake. He wasn't sure if they still greeted each other that way on the surface, but it appeared they did. The return greetings were not very enthusiastic, however.

"Bishop, this is Deiondre," Leo said, introducing the black woman sitting closest to the door. "Her husband is Chikae, the leader of the Brotherhood, and this," he motioned to the white woman, sitting as far away as she could, "is Jackie. She is married to Jim Crow Robinson, the leader of the Brigade."

"It is so good to meet you both," Elu said. He found a stool to sit on, making a triangle with the two women, with Leo sort of in the middle. "I am Elu Wilussit, the bishop of Chicago. My wife is Matilda and we have a grandson we are raising by the name of Matthew. I'd love to hear about your families."

Elu hoped to connect with these women around something they all shared and what he hoped would be something dear to them.

Deiondre answered first: "Well, bishop, Chikae and I have two children, Kanesha is 10 and her brother Kentay is 12."

"Ah, a boy and a girl! That is so nice! What sort of things do they like to do? Do they have any chance of going to school?"

"Well, there isn't much to do in the city these days, of

course. I don't know about the tunnels. Brother Leo says you live in the tunnels. Our kids learn from us, and I try to teach them the basics, you know. We have some books. We do reading and math and all. They play baseball a lot. That's about all there is to do, though, I'm afraid."

"Ah, that is nice! I've read a lot about baseball, but you're right, in the tunnels we don't have room for that, unfortunately. What about you, Jackie? Do you have children?"

"Yeah, we got two, too. Tommy is the oldest. He's eight. Leah is seven. Same for us. They don't get to do much, you know."

That seemed to dry up the conversation for a few moments, which became a bit uncomfortable. Then Elu jumped in again.

"Well, I really thank you for coming here to meet, today."

"Yeah," said Jackie. "What's this all about? Brother Leo wasn't real clear. Frankly, I wouldn't even be here, except I trust Leo. He's harmless and a nice guy and the kids like him. I gotta tell you, though, I'm a bit nervous about being here in this hole in the ground, with all you "colored" folks!"

"I understand," said Elu. Before he could add anything else, Deiondre spoke up.

"Just like your kind, Jackie! Don't trust anybody that looks different! If I were you, I'd be more worried about that husband of yours!"

"Just you be quiet about my husband! He's a good man! Not anything like that…well, the one you have!" replied Jackie.

Elu decided he better take control of the conversation before it came to blows. There was clearly a lot of distrust and dislike between these two.

"Well, it's natural to distrust someone you don't know, and I think it's human nature, also, to worry about someone who may seem so different. I'm not usually considered scary! I'm just an old man, you know! A lot like Brother Leo! But, this is the first time we've met, and with the uncertainties, I'm sure it can make anyone a bit uneasy. That's why I'm so happy you were both brave enough to come here today."

That seemed to help. The women were both looking at Elu, and they quit harping at each other, at least for the moment.

"I am from the tunnels, as Brother Leo has said. In the tunnels, we rarely ever come to the surface. We have all we need, after all. But, we do hear the fighting. Nearly every day, we hear explosions. It worries us. It worries me. I think, frankly, it worries God! I worry about you and your families. It can't be easy raising children in a situation like this. In fact, I...I lost my own daughter and her husband, when an explosive from the surface fell down into our tunnel once, several years ago." Elu had to choke out these words. He wiped his eyes and blew his nose, as he thought to himself that it may well have been one of these two women, or their husbands, who actually launched that bomb. He soon recovered, though and asked them: "Do you worry about your kids?"

Both of the women nodded just a bit. Elu thought he could see a tear on Deiondre's cheek. Jackie was clearing her throat. Elu went on.

"Well, ladies, the only reason I'm here, is to see if I can help. I want to do whatever I can to help end the fighting. Wouldn't that be wonderful, if the fighting could end and you never again had to worry about the safety of your boys and girls?"

"I don't know, bishop. It's been going on for too long. I don't think it'll ever end. How could it? We hate each other!" Deiondre stated, briefly glancing over at Jackie.

After a pause, Elu addressed Jackie: "Jackie, what do you think?"

"I think this is a waste of time! And, I think it's dangerous for us to be here. If anybody sees us here, there could be hell to pay!"

"Yes, it is dangerous. All the more reason to try to change things. And, again, I'm very impressed at your bravery coming here," offered Elu. "Do you think it's been going on too long to stop it, Jackie?"

"We hate each other for good reasons, bishop! I lost my parents and two brothers to those…! I'll never forget that!" She answered.

"We've all lost people, Jackie! I lost a sister, and my parents, and two cousins, and I can't count how many more! All because you people won't share anything! You want to just wipe us all out!"

Before Elu could say anything else, Jackie jumped up from her chair, and ran at Deiondre. Deiondre jumped up to defend herself. Elu was expecting something like this. He quickly concentrated and dropped the two of them out of the time gap. They froze in place. Only he and Leo were still aware of what was going on.

Leo was speechless. He sat there with his eyes bulging out and his mouth open.

"What happened!" he gasped.

"Leo, my friend, this is something you need to keep quiet about. I have a special spiritual gift, the Lord has given me, to do this. They will not know I did it, but it can keep them from hurting each other," Elu explained.

Elu got up from his stool, and asked Leo to help him. They physically separated the two women, moving them to opposite corners of the room. Then, Elu stationed Leo in front of Deiondre and he stood in front of Jackie.

"OK, Leo, get ready. Here we go!" and Elu let the two slip back into intra-time.

"What! What's going on!" shouted Jackie. "What are you doing standing here? Where is that black …!"

"Please, Jackie, calm down. Leo and I have separated you. We will not allow violence here. Please, sit down and let's talk."

On the other end of the room, Deiondre was wondering the same things. She watched the two churchmen very carefully. When the two were separated, they ended up on different sides of the room. Now, Jackie was closest to the door.

"Sit, hell! I'm outta here! Don't follow me! It would be bad for you and for me both!"

With that, Jackie was out the door and up the stairs.

Chapter 19

Deiondre waited a while after Jackie left and then she departed, also. Elu and Leo were left alone and they discussed the meeting.

"I'm sorry, bishop. It didn't go well, at all!"

"Leo, it's OK. I didn't expect anything different. We simply need to keep at it, that's all. At least I have now met these women and we have begun to form a relationship. It was a heroic effort on your part to even get them both here at the same time! Well done, my friend!"

"Thank you, your excellency. But, I wish I could have done more."

"Do you see them, or their children, at all regularly, Leo?"

"Not regularly, exactly, but probably a time or two every week. I try to make myself present. What I usually do is wander the streets and meet the kids as they are out playing sports or something. I just sit and watch and they come to talk to me at times. That's how I met their mothers. They will, rarely, sit and talk to me, too."

"I think that's perfect. Keep doing it. I don't want them to think we have given up and I don't want them to think your visits were only to get them here to talk to me, either. Just keep spending the time, showing them that you care."

"I will, of course. When will I see you again, bishop?"

"Leo, I think you and I should plan to meet regularly. I need to get out of the tunnel every so often, anyway. What I can do is plan to meet you here once a week or so. Would that work, do you think?"

"Of course, excellency! That would be wonderful!"

"And, Leo, one other thing. Especially now that we have

begun at least something with the factions up here, I think we need to have a way for you to contact me if you need to. You would always be welcome anytime, of course, but with this situation going on, it's probably more critical."

"Yes, bishop, I agree. How should we work that?"

"Well, the best way is for me to simply show you where our tunnel is. You can come and get me whenever you need something. Would you like to come home with me now?"

"That would be great, bishop! I'm ready to go!"

Elu took the precaution of entering intra-time and bringing Leo along with him into the gap, as they left the friary. He didn't want to risk having anyone from the factions see where their tunnel was, and he wasn't inclined to be "jumped" by anyone as they traveled, either. He led Leo back down State Street and across the river to Wacker Drive. They turned east and walked for a couple blocks to the overhang at the stairway entrance.

"Well, here we are, Leo. It's down here, several stories down, in fact."

"I know this place, bishop! I've never been down the stairs, but I have been passed it many times. There is nothing here to indicate that anyone lives down there!"

"No, there isn't, Leo. It was well chosen by my predecessor. Also, of course, no one from the tunnels has been up to the surface for several centuries, until now!"

The two slowly descended the stairs, and were finally on the upper tunnel level. They were still in the time gap in case any of the tunnel people happened to be there. Elu wanted to do a more controlled introduction to his own people, when appropriate. That time was coming closer and closer, he realized, but he wanted to avoid an awkward chance encounter.

Leo marveled at the huge sundial in the middle of that level. He had never seen anything quite like it before.

"This is where we get our fundamental time measurement. We have several hourglasses in strategic spots but we use this to set everything," Elu explained.

The most impressive sight on that level, according to Leo, however, was the cathedral itself. It was a dwarf church, in many ways, especially compared to the former glory of Holy Name Cathedral, where Leo lived. But, of course, Leo only had pictures of that and they were pretty faded. This "cathedral" was small, but it was still a large enough space to hold several hundred congregants. Elu could fit the entire tunnel population at once in the pews. The ceiling was very low for a church of any kind. It was also dark and lit with only a few lights, with some optional torches. The community had worked long and hard to decorate the place, though, and Leo found it breathtaking. He was a bit reticent to approach the altar and would not go anywhere near the tabernacle.

"I'm simply not worthy, your excellency! I'm a simple friar. I've only received one sacrament in my entire life, you know. We haven't had priests for generations and so I've only been baptized."

"Leo, it never occurred to me, but of course! Oh, my! You have never received the Eucharist or been confirmed! We will have to correct that, my friend! We should plan on doing both of those things very soon!"

Leo looked like he was going to cry, right there in the sanctuary. He dropped to his knees, and thanked Elu profusely. Elu was rather embarrassed but accepted Leo's thanks graciously. Finally, he was able to get the friar back onto his feet.

"Leo, it's midafternoon. Let me bring you over to meet my wife Matilda. You must stay for dinner with us. She will insist on it, you know."

Leo was almost speechless. He had never had such an experience like this his entire life. He mutely followed his bishop to the other end of the level to the bishop's dwelling.

"Matilda, here's the man you have wanted to meet. Brother Leo, my wife Matilda."

"Oh, Brother Leo! I've heard such wonderful things about you! It's so good to meet you!" Matilda rushed to give the friar a hug.

Leo was overwhelmed again. He had no idea how to address the wife of a bishop. He had never been taught that, and realized there probably was no particular formula. Despite all he had read and learned, this was a new thing in the church. He decided it was a good thing.

"My dear, Mrs…bishop?? It is good to meet you as well."

Matilda laughed, and Elu chuckled.

"Please, Leo, you can call me Matilda or simply Mattie. We are not very formal down here. Will you stay for supper? I'm about to get it going."

"See what I told you, Leo? She's a good cook, too!" offered Elu.

"Thank you so much! I must get back to my friary, but I suppose I can leave after we eat! Thank you!"

Elu and Leo retired briefly to the study, and talked a bit about the surface people, and Elu's plans to reveal the story to his own parishioners. Soon, Matilda called them to eat.

"Who's that?" blurted Matthew when Leo appeared at the dinner table.

"Matthew, I want you to meet a good friend of mine, Brother Leo. Leo, this is our grandson, Matthew."

"It's good to meet you, Matthew."

"Where are you from? I've never seen you before!"

"Brother Leo is from up on the surface, Matthew."

"You're one of those fighters?" Exclaimed the boy.

"No, no, I'm not, but I do know them, and I try to help them to see that they don't need to fight any more. It's a hard job!" said Leo.

"Now, Matthew, Brother Leo is a guest, but he is here on sort of a secret mission. You remember what a secret mission is, don't you?"

"Yeah, you're supposed to sneak around and hide under things. Why aren't you hiding?"

"Well, in a sense, I am hiding, Matthew. I'm hiding here with you and your grandparents, but just for a little bit, then I'll be going back up the stairs."

"Is it safe up there?"

"Well, it is, if you're careful and know what you're doing. I wouldn't recommend it for anyone else, right now."

"Matthew, just don't mention anything about Brother Leo to your friends right now. I want it to be a surprise. We'll talk about it Sunday at Mass, then you can tell your friends you knew all about it. How do you think that'll be?"

"I like surprises! I won't say anything."

"Are you sure about announcing it at Mass, dear? There may be quite a commotion about it. Will Leo be there?"

"Now that I have met some of the combatants on the surface, I think I have to, Mattie. And, I think we should NOT have Leo there the first time we talk about it. I want people to start to get comfortable with it before they meet him. What do you think? Will that work?"

"That's probably a good idea. We knew the time would come when we had to tell everybody what you are doing. I'll be a bit nervous until then, I have to say."

Then all four said a prayer for the upcoming announcement, including it in their meal prayer. Leo enjoyed the first home cooked meal of his life, and then quickly left to get back to his friary before dark. After dark it was a bit more dangerous, besides there was hardly any light to navigate by.

Chapter 20

Leo arrived back at the friary just as the sun was going down. As he walked in, he heard a noise coming from inside. Then a faint voice.

"Leo…is it…you?"

"Yes, it's me, who's there?"

Then he saw her. It was Jackie, but he almost didn't recognize her. Of course, the light was bad, but her face was swollen, and there were blood streaks around her forehead. She tried to get up from where she was lying, but had trouble doing that.

"Jackie! Oh, my God, what happened?"

"They found out, Leo. They found out I had been here and that I had met with you and that black woman."

"Oh, no, Jackie! Here, let me help you."

Leo helped her onto his sleeping platform. He didn't really have a bed, but he slept on a wooden platform that had once been part of the cathedral above. Jackie had been lying on the floor. He ran to get a damp cloth and began to wash her face.

"Where else are you hurt?" he asked her.

"Just my face. I think I twisted my ankle trying to get away. Oh, and my shoulder, here," she motioned to her right arm. "They were holding me and it got twisted, I think."

"Did Jim Crow do this to you, Jackie?" Leo asked.

"No, he wouldn't do it himself. But he ordered it…I can't go back, Leo. They'll kill me. Not only that, but they'll kill my kids, too…I don't know what to do!"

Leo's damp cloth became mingled with Jackie's tears.

"I wish I had more to help you with. We need to get you out of here. You know they'll come for you when the sun comes up."

"I know. But I have nowhere else to go."

"I know somewhere we can go. But, it's hard to get there in the dark. We should leave just as soon as we can see in the morning."

"Do you think it's safe to wait that long? Where are we going, anyway?"

"We'll go to the bishop's tunnel. I've been there. You'll be safe there. And, we have to wait. You aren't in any shape to go right now, anyway. At least rest overnight."

"I don't know, Leo. They'll kill the bishop, too, if they know I went there. I shouldn't have come here. They'll kill you, too, you know."

"It doesn't matter what they do to me, Jackie. We'll get you out of here to safety, first thing in the morning."

Jackie truly wasn't in any shape to travel. She was hurt badly, and seemed to Leo that she was drifting in and out of consciousness, even as she talked to him. He could only hope she would improve at least some overnight.

Leo spent all night awake, watching for anyone trying to get to them. He put out his torch for the night, hoping they wouldn't be able to find the place in the dark. He couldn't sleep anyway since he had given Jackie his only place to sleep. There was nowhere else to sleep in the tiny room he had.

Finally, the black Chicago night began to lighten, almost imperceptibly. Leo realized he had no choice. He woke Jackie up. She was still pretty groggy, and she limped badly on that ankle. But, they had to get started. It was hard getting up the few stairs out of the friary, and Leo began to worry about getting her down the steep and long stairway at the tunnel.

The two of them made very slow progress along State Street. It seemed to take forever, and Leo was certain they were taking at least twice as long as he and Elu had taken the evening before. Leo prayed the whole way, but still expected to see hoodlums jump out from behind every corner and rubbish pile along the way.

Soon, they were at the river. They crossed the bridge, with Leo practically dragging Jackie the whole length. He was in a hurry to cross, knowing that the chances of being attacked by the White Power Brigade would be much less on the south side. Then another several blocks and finally he had brought his charge to the canopy protecting the stairway. He was right about the stairs. It was very hard to carry Jackie, even going down. She was almost dead weight. Leo made it to the first level, with several to go before he reached the occupied portion. He decided this was far enough, she was safe for now. He laid her down and tucked her in a bit, into the blocked tunnel on that level. Then he hurried the rest of the way alone.

Matilda was alone in the bishop's dwelling when Leo burst in.

"Mattie, where is the bishop! We have an emergency!"

"Oh, Leo, oh my, he's at the cathedral. He's about to start morning Mass. What is it?"

"One of the wives we met with yesterday, she's been beaten badly. I could only get her down about one level down the stairway. We need some men to help me get her down to safety!"

Matilda didn't hesitate. She ran out the door, pulling Leo with her.

"Come on, Leo. If Elu has started Mass, hopefully some others will be there."

The two of them hurried over to the cathedral, and into the sacristy, from the side door that pretty much only Elu used. Elu was in his robes, but hadn't begun Mass yet.

"Elu, come, quickly, we have an injured woman on the stairway!" Matilda yelled as soon as she saw her husband. Elu left with her and Leo right away, not even bothering to remove his robes.

The three of them quickly reached the level where Jackie was still hidden. She was very groggy and they could tell she barely recognized them. Between the three of them, they managed to get her down the rest of the way and into the bishop's dwelling. They laid her on the couch, and Mattie got some clean clothes and water and again bathed her face.

"Elu, go, get Jodie! She'll have to come up here."

Elu nodded and quickly left. Leo stayed to help Matilda. Soon, Elu was back with Jodie, who brought along her emergency medical kit. She began to tend to the woman's wounds. After some tense moments, Jodie told them she was sure Jackie would recover. She had been beaten and likely had a concussion, but there was no sign of anything worse. She simply needed to rest.

"Elu, who is this?" Asked Matilda.

"This is Jackie, Jackie Robinson, the wife of Jim Crow Robinson, the leader of the white faction on the surface. I suspect she was beaten because she was seen meeting with us, and especially with the woman from the black faction."

"Yes, that's what she told me," interjected Leo. "Are you sure she's going to be alright?"

Jodie nodded. "Yes, she should be, but she does need rest. I'll give you a list of things to do."

"Well," stated Elu, "this changes our timeline for announcements, doesn't it? Jodie, would you please keep this quiet for right now? I'll begin the process to have a community-wide gathering this afternoon. Things are likely going to become more complicated very soon, and people need to know what's going on."

Chapter 21

"Please, let's quiet down, now and get started. I need everyone's attention," Elu shouted over the din in the cathedral. He was standing in front of the altar. It was a slightly raised platform. The body of the church, the "nave", had been constructed with a slight incline, so everyone could see him. Over the years, there had been very carefully constructed baffles added to the ceiling and the sides of the large room, in very astute ways, so that the sound would echo from that very spot. It was like one of those ancient basilicas, constructed so that sound would carry well from the central podium.

"My friends," said Elu, after the place had quieted down, "a problem has arisen. It may be considered an opportunity, as well, but first let us pray that the Lord will help us to act appropriately in this matter."

Elu then led the congregation in a short prayer, asking for wisdom and for peace. When he was done, he continued.

"We have all, over the years, been very concerned about the fighting on the surface. We hear their explosions almost daily, some near and some far away. We've always been a little bit on edge, hoping their hostilities wouldn't reach us down in our refuge, here. Earlier today, those hostilities did reach us. One of the women from the white faction has come to us, badly beaten because she bravely attempted to work to end the fighting. She is currently being cared for in my dwelling by Matilda and Jodie. We expect her to recover but she is in no shape to meet anyone at this time."

This announcement caused a flurry of excitement and a loud rumble of voices. Elu had to motion again for silence.

"This woman, whose name is Jackie, came to us through the care of a man I had previously met. This man is not connected with either of the factions, but he lives on the surface as a Franciscan friar. Brother Leo is his name and he is a hermit, living in the ruins of the ancient Holy Name Cathedral, the former Cathedral of Chicago. He's the one who brought Jackie to our tunnels, to escape certain death at the hands of her own people."

This engendered even more spontaneous talking and gesticulating by the crowd. Elu let this go on for a while, and when it died down, he continued.

"There is more, of course, but that is the gist of the problem we face at this time. I think it would be most appropriate now to respond to any questions."

"How did this friar know to bring her to our tunnels?" asked one man.

"As I said, I had met Brother Leo previously. He has been working among the surface people, simply giving them spiritual advice, and trying to befriend their children. His situation is tenuous and I extended an invitation to him to seek asylum in our tunnels if needed. He declined that offer, because he felt he had a mission from God to be with the people above. However, he had no way to care for this woman's injuries, and so he rightfully brought her to us."

"Bishop, how did you meet Brother Leo?"

"As you all know, I have wanted for many years to somehow find a way to bring Christ to the people above us, to try to end their constant fighting. Recently, I found a way to surreptitiously scout out the situation up there. I can assure you it was done very discreetly, and, until now, there was no way for anyone on the surface to know I had been there, or where we were hiding, or even that we existed."

"What are we going to do now? Surely, the surface fighters will find us, and now we're all in danger!" proclaimed someone else.

"I believe Brother Leo acted appropriately. We have to offer asylum and comfort to anyone who asks. I also believe the

Lord will protect us, but we do need to be cautious. I have several ideas, but I would welcome any thoughts anyone else has."

"Bishop," asked a woman in the front row. Elu recognized her. It was Jennilu. She was often at odds with how Elu organized and ran things. "I am surprised that you would put us all at risk, going up to the surface like that! Now, look what you've done!"

"Jennilu, I appreciate your concern. It was a calculated risk, but, frankly, these factions were going to find us eventually, anyway. The more they destroy the surface, the more they will be looking for avenues of escape, just as our ancestors did. I believed at the time, and I still do, that our best chance of survival was to engage them, and try to end the combat on the surface. I understand that some might not agree, but I do believe it was the most appropriate thing to do."

"Well," she continued, "now you've brought them down on us sooner than they would have. And who else did you consult before you did this."

"Jenni," offered Elu, "the surface combatants have not "come down on us" at this point, and I am not sure they will. However, I still believe it was the right thing to do."

Elu pointedly did not respond to the question of whom he consulted, since it was only God and Adeevan. That would invite too much scoffing on the one hand and questions on the other.

"What do you think we should do, bishop?" Asked someone else.

"Well, first of all, I would suggest we set a watch. We should have at least one person watching the stairway at all times. In fact, Richard LH is out there right now, watching for us. We will need to set up a process for notification if anyone is seen trying to get down here. Secondly, I would suggest we set up some barriers along the various levels of the stairway. They don't need to be much, but enough to give the impression that the stairway is blocked. If nothing else, that would give us time to respond to anyone trying to get down here."

That seemed to end the questions for the moment, and so Elu asked those who would be willing to be part of the watch committee to stay behind. He also promised to let everyone meet Jackie and Brother Leo very soon, when it was appropriate, and after she had recovered, of course. The watch committee was soon formed and a watch schedule set up. Several families volunteered to help set up "junk piles" on each level of the stairway, to be sort of a "reverse decoy" for anyone attempting to venture into the tunnels.

Chapter 22

Back home, Elu checked in on Jackie, and collected Leo.

"Leo, I think it would be a good idea for you to come around with me and meet some of our people. They have all heard about you now, and I think they should meet you," he said to the friar.

"Bishop, a good idea, but I am afraid of being away from the friary too long. I'm worried about Deiondre. What if something like this happened to her, too? I need to be there for her."

"I understand, Leo, but let's at least visit a few folks. I'd like to start with the school, I think. You'll enjoy that."

"Alright, your excellency. I think I can spare some time."

The two of them sauntered down the ramp to the next level and were soon at the classroom. Class had been disrupted by the meeting in the cathedral earlier, and so they had re-gathered to just complete the daily lessons. The tradition in the tunnels was to always bring the children to a special community meeting, so they had all been there and heard about Brother Leo.

Miss Theresa saw them at the door and welcomed them in.

"Class, our bishop is here, with a special visitor! Come in. I bet this is Brother Leo!"

The class all stood to greet the bishop, as they normally did. After they all quieted down and were sitting down again, Elu sat on his customary stool, and addressed the group.

"Boys and girls, were you all at the meeting this afternoon?"

All the heads nodded and one little girl raised her hand.

"Yes, Stephanie?"

"I was there bishop, with my mom and dad. I didn't understand it all but is this Brother Leo?"

"Yes, Stephanie," Elu said with a grin. "This is my friend, Brother Leo. Everyone say hi to Brother Leo."

All the children stood again, and greeted Leo. Then they all sat back down. Several hands went up.

"Well, Leo, I think they want to ask you some things. Is that OK with you?"

"Of course, bishop! I'd love to answer their questions!"

"Where do you live?" one boy asked.

"Well, I live in a place called a friary. I used to live there with several other friars, but now I'm all by myself. It's on the surface, quite a ways from here."

"What's a fry-ur-ee" asked one girl.

"Well, a friary is where friars live. The word friar is an old word meaning brother. We lived as brothers, all serving the Lord Jesus."

"What happened to all the others?" someone asked.

"Well, they were all a lot older than me, and they all got to the end of their lives. They are all buried in our little cemetery by the friary, now."

"What's a semi-taree", someone asked.

"Now, children, let's concentrate a bit on Brother Leo. Who wants to know what he does on the surface?"

Everyone raised their hands, and so Leo explained.

"Well, the Lord has given me a special ministry to the people on the surface. You all know, I think, that they're angry with each other, and they fight a lot. It's hard on the children. They have children, too, you know, just like all of you. I try to spend time with them and help them deal with all the fighting. I do that with some of the adults, too, but mostly the kids."

"What are the kids like? Are they like us?"

"Oh, yes, kids are kids, you know! They play games together, and have fun, just like you. There are two differences. They don't get to go to school, like you do. Their moms teach them some things. The other thing is that the kids from one area are not allowed to play with the kids from the other area. They're taught to hate the others. That's one thing I try to teach them, that they are really all the same."

"That's sad," said one little girl.

"What kind of games do they play?" asked another.

"Well, they have more room to play than you do down here, you know. They often play baseball."

That unleashed another stream of questions and Leo found himself about to teach the kids all about baseball and what it was and how it was played. There were lots more questions, but Leo was getting tired, and Elu and Miss Theresa decided it was time for the questions to end, so they could get back to their lessons. Everyone stood up again to say goodbye to Brother Leo and the bishop, and they left.

"Leo, I'm sorry that took so long! We may need to do the other visiting later. I'd like to show you our farm, though, before you leave. I think you'd enjoy that," Elu proposed.

"Oh, yes, bishop! You have a farm?" Leo responded.

"We sure do, down all the way, though. It's a bit of a walk, and harder coming back up, of course. We're not young men, anymore, but I think we can get it done!"

On the way to the farm, of course, they ran into several other folks, who stopped to meet Leo and chat for a bit. They did finally make it to the farm, and Leo was very impressed.

"Bishop, is this from the river? It's amazing!"

"Yes, Leo, we think this is an underground tributary of the main stem of the Chicago River above. I don't know if it is a natural tributary, or if it had something to do with the construction of the tunnels, but it was here when our ancestors first occupied the tunnels. Here's Jodie. You met her upstairs. She's not only our medic, but she also runs the farm and is our veterinarian."

"Hello, Leo, how's our patient upstairs? I was just about to go back up to see," asked Jodie.

"She's better, I think, thanks to you. This is an impressive place here!" Leo marveled.

"Let me show you!"

Jodie led Leo all around, and showed him the chicken area and the hydroponics.

"We feed the entire place with what we grow here. The river supplies our water, although the guys have to haul it up in large casks to each level. The sewage from all the dwellings empties into the river downstream, behind that wall."

After the farm tour, Leo and Elu hurried back up the ramps to the bishop's place, and checked on Jackie, before Leo left for the day. She was doing ok, and Leo promised to be back the next day, to continue meeting the tunnel residents.

Chapter 23

"What are you doing, dear?" asked Matilda.

"Mattie, thank you for all you did for me. I can't stay here, though. I have to get back," answered Jackie.

It was the next morning, and Jackie was feeling more or less back to normal. Her face was still swollen some and she had a black eye. She also walked with a bit of a limp.

"Of course, you can stay here! You are welcome to stay as long as you need to," Mattie replied.

Just then, Elu and Leo walked in. Elu was coming back from morning Mass, and he had met Leo as he came back down the stairway.

"What's going on?" asked Elu.

"Bishop, thank you for your care and thank you, Brother Leo, but I have to get back home to my family."

"Jackie, are you sure about this?"

"Yes, I miss my kids and I don't know what they'll do without me!"

"Jackie," said Elu softly, "I don't think it's safe. If we have to, we can bring your kids here. You're welcome to stay and become part of our community!"

"Oh, no, I couldn't do that!" she replied.

"What're you going to do, Jackie?" asked Leo. "You know as well as I do that Jim Crow will have you killed if you show up there again. Even if you found your kids, you couldn't stay with the Brigade anymore. Where would you go?"

"I don't know...all I know is, I have to get back to my kids!" Jackie made this last statement in a bit of a huff, not looking at any of them, trying to hide her tears. She walked resolutely toward the door, but then wobbled and fell over. Elu and Leo were able to grab her and help her gently to the floor. She then sat in a heap and wept openly.

Elu knelt down to her.

"Jackie, you're in no shape to go up there. Let's do this. Leo and I will go and bring your children down here to you. Leo knows them, and I can help."

Leo also stooped down and nodded. He rested his hand on Jackie's shoulder. Then the two of them helped her back up and onto the couch again. She sat in the middle of it and held her head in her hands for a long moment.

"Then what?" she asked. "What do we do then?"

"We'll cross that bridge when we come to it, Jackie, but you and your kids are always welcome to simply stay here. But, let's get them down here first and then we'll see."

Jackie nodded almost imperceptibly, and Mattie sat down next to her and took her hands in hers.

"It'll be alright. You and I will wait here together, while the men go get them. What are their names, Jackie?"

"Tommie and Leah. He's 8, she's 7."

"We're off right now, then, to get them," declared Elu, as he and Leo went out the door.

"Bishop, this may be a difficult and dangerous mission. We need to have a plan," Leo said, as they made their way up the stairway.

"Yes, and I have one, Leo. Do you remember when we separated the two women in the friary, as they were about to attack one another?"

"Yes, excellency, it was very strange. You mentioned something about a "gift" you had. What was that?"

"Well, it's exactly what we're going to do now. To simplify it, basically, I have the ability to stop time, and to bring anyone I want with me into a "time gap", so to speak. Watch this, now."

The two of them were at the last landing on the stairway before the surface. The street level was visible to them from under the outside canopy.

"Stop here a moment, Leo. Look up there. You can see some things blowing around in the wind. There are even a few birds flying around. See those?"

Leo nodded.

"Now, watch them," Elu said, as he concentrated and brought himself and Leo into the time gap. Suddenly everything stopped. There were even a few small birds caught in mid-air, that they could see through the canopy opening.

"Ohhh!" Exclaimed Leo, as he crossed himself. "They have just stopped! The birds are floating, like, hovering, or something! How did you do that!"

"Well, I'm not exactly sure I could explain it myself, but it's essentially a contemplation technique. We'll stay in this time gap, now, until we get back. Let's go!"

Elu started back up the last stair level, and Leo, after a momentary hesitation, followed quickly. They emerged from under the canopy, and Leo motioned for them to head toward the lake. Soon, they were traversing the river, and then into Brigade territory, the old Chicago neighborhood of Streeterville. Leo knew it well. He knew exactly where the Brigade children normally played their games. Sure enough, they came up on a clearing in one of the side streets. The place had been cleared and a baseball field marked out. There were about a dozen kids, apparently in the middle of a game, but, of course, frozen in time.

"Here we are, bishop. That's Tommy there, at bat, and, Leah should be here someplace. Oh, yes, there she is, over on the third base line."

Elu wasn't all that familiar with baseball terminology, so he followed Leo. They came up to Tommy first. The two men stood facing the boy, one on either side as he straddled "home plate", which was a flat rock. They stayed a bit away, to try to avoid startling him.

Suddenly, Tommy came "alive". He saw them standing there and lowered his bat.

"What! What's going on! What are you doing here?" the boy said, and then ran toward Leo, with a menacing look on his face, and the bat raised over his head. He abruptly stopped, and was again frozen in time.

"Leo, I think he's angry with you. I'm afraid he's trying to attack you with that stick…er…bat!"

"He might blame me for his mother being gone."

Elu walked over and took the bat from Tommy's hands. Then, he positioned himself between Leo and the boy, holding the bat crosswise in front of him.

"Whoa, what happened!" the boy exclaimed as he suddenly came alive, again. He almost ran into Elu, but was able to stop himself before he did. He looked at the bat, and then at his own hands, and then just stood there staring.

Leo came around from the side, and said: "Tommy, we've come to bring you to your mother. We don't want to harm you."

Tommy jumped at Leo, who caught him and was able to hold his arms and avoid any blows.

"My mom's dead! You killed her! I hate you!" he exclaimed.

Leo held the boy close. "No, Tommy, she's not. She's OK. Let us take you to where she is. Let's get your sister, too."

"You just want to kill us both!" Although his words were still very defiant, Tommy was starting to soften. He was struggling less, and he had tears in his eyes.

"Which one is Leah?" asked Elu. Leo pointed to the sister, who was only about halfway down from third base, probably about ten feet away, on their small-scale diamond. Elu looked at her, and, briefly nodding his head, she came alive also.

"Leah!" called Leo. "Come here! We're taking you to your mother. She's alive and well!"

Leah hesitated, but then, seeing her brother in Leo's arms, came running up, assuming he was being abducted.

"No! Don't take Tommy, too!" She ran up and began to hit Leo, but Elu grabbed her arms, and held them.

"Leah, Tommy, you know me," Leo began. "You trust me, I know you do. You know I wouldn't harm anyone, especially your mother. I won't hurt you, either. Your mother is OK, but she misses you both. Come with us, and we'll take you to her."

Leah looked up at Leo, unsure what to do. Then, she looked over her shoulder, and called out to a man who was sitting watching the game. Leo had not seen him there earlier.

"Daddy, what should we do?"

"Oh, my, bishop, that's Jim Crow sitting right over there!"

Elu looked and saw a shortish, young man, dressed in jeans and a sleeveless t-shirt. His head was shaved and Elu could see quite a number of tattoos, although from a distance, he couldn't make out any of their shapes. He appeared to be smoking something.

"Daddy! What should we do?" Leah called again.

"Leah," Leo offered gently, "he can't hear you. He can't see you right now, either. He doesn't even know we're here. He won't see you go. It's safer this way. He'll be OK, we just need you to come to see your mother, right now."

Leah studied her father for a bit, then turned back to Leo.

"She's really OK?" she asked.

"Yes, dear, she is. Let's go see her, alright?"

Leah nodded, and the four of them ventured off the baseball field, and down the street back towards the river. As they approached the bridge, Tommy stopped, and wouldn't go any further.

"We aren't allowed on that bridge. The blacks'll kill us! They're monsters!"

"No one will harm you, Tommy. The bishop and I will protect you," Leo told him.

Tommy glanced over at Elu and then to Leo. He took Leah's hand, and then very cautiously started across the bridge. Soon, they were across and hurried down Wacker Drive to the stairway. Leah and Tommy both were very tentative descending the stairs, clearly very much in awe and quite fearful. Once the group had reached the upper level of the tunnels, Elu let them all out of the time gap.

"Bishop, Brother Leo, looks like you were successful! Wow, that was fast! You're back already!" Richard LH was there, on the watch. He smiled at Tommy and Leah, while both of the kids clung more closely to Leo.

They walked into the bishop's dwelling, and were both surprised to actually see their mother sitting on the cot with Mattie. To the two women, it seemed like the small rescue team had only been gone a few minutes. But, they ignored that small fact, as the two children reunited with their mother.

Chapter 24

"Bishop, I'm sorry if I disturbed you!" Leo said. He had come to the cathedral to pray before going back to his friary. He had been helping Jackie and her kids get settled in a vacant dwelling just near the classroom, and was on his way to the stairway. He was surprised to see Elu sitting in the sanctuary.

"No, Leo, it's not a bother. How are you doing? Did you get our family settled in?"

"Yes, excellency. They were very impressed with the accommodations, I must say!"

"Well, you should join us, too, you know!"

"Thank you, bishop, maybe I will, but not right now. There is still work to do up top, you know."

"Yes, there is…I certainly hope you do a better job of it than I'm doing, my friend…" Elu's voice trailed off, as he stared at his hands.

"What do you mean, bishop?"

"Well, Leo, all I seem to have managed so far is to get Jackie beat up, and to divide their family. I'm not sure any of it was worth the risks we took."

"It looks bad, now, bishop, but frankly, none of that was your fault, and I'm not sure some of it might not have happened anyway. There are great stresses in that Brigade and those families. Besides, I always try to remember what our old prior used to say: "if you do your best, but bad things happen, remember, there are bad people, and they do bad things, and it's not your fault. Just be faithful, and all will go according to His plan.""

"Good words, Leo, good advice. But, I would add when bad things happen, it can sometimes be a learning experience. What could we have done better, and what should we do better next time? It is His plan, I'm sure, for something to be done and I'm also sure we're part of that plan. We, or, at least I, need to be more attentive to the Spirit and more careful."

"That may well be, but, we do have some opportunities, here."

"Tell me about them, brother. I'd love to hear about opportunities."

"Well, we have JCR's kids...sorry, JCR is what that call Jim Crow Robinson...we have his family. He will wonder what happened, and he will blame either the Brotherhood, or us, and likely both. That'll stir things up, and we may be able to use that as leverage, in some way. We just need to figure out how."

"Do you think this will stir up hostilities above?"

"Oh, I'm sure it will. They don't need much of an excuse, anyway."

"What do they usually do if something like this were to happen? Would they plan out something, be secretive about it, or just charge the other side?"

"JCR can be impulsive, but when it comes to something like this, he would likely plan some kind of revenge. They would not be looking for a rescue operation. They would assume their people were already dead, and so they would take their time and scout out a counter-attack."

"Is there any way that you can find out what they are planning, or when?"

"Oh, certainly. It's not hard. They think they are very clandestine about things, but I have, let's say, some ways to find out things."

"If you were to find out their plans, what kind of lead time would we have to do something about it?"

"Oh, easily several hours, probably a full day in advance."

"Leo, that is helpful. Please, be very careful. Don't get yourself into something you can't handle. But, if you find out any-thing, let me know as soon as you can."

"I can do that, bishop. No problem. As soon as I know something, you'll know it!"

"That may be the opportunity we're looking for. Thanks, Leo!"

Leo asked again for Elu's blessing and then left for the evening. He headed back to his friary, and began to consider the best way to get the information the bishop needed. The Bri-gade would be on high alert, but Leo was pretty confident that he could slip in and out and get what he wanted. He had done it many times in the past.

As Leo headed for the stairs, Elu walked with him halfway, then headed home. As he walked into the dwelling, he saw Mat-tie and Jackie on the sofa, talking. Tommy and Leah were play-ing with Matthew in the corner.

"Elu, you're back already," said Matilda. "Jackie and I were just talking about her new apartment."

"I hope it's OK, Jackie. I'm sorry we didn't have time to fix it up much. How are you doing?"

"I'm much better, bishop. Thank you so much for every-thing. This whole place is so much nicer than anything we have on the surface. I don't know how to thank you, you've all been so nice..." At this point, Jackie broke down a bit, and couldn't continue. Mattie patted her hand, and Elu pulled over a chair.

"Jackie, it's not a problem. We're honored to do it. If you're up to it, I do have a question or two."

Jackie blew her nose and nodded, "I'm OK, really. What kind of questions?"

"Now that Tommy and Leah are here, what do you think might happen on the surface? Do you think your people, your... husband...might...do anything bad?"

"I've tried not to think about it, but, yeah, he probably will."

"If you're not up to it, Jackie…"

"No, no, I'm fine, but you're right. My husband is a good man, mostly. He can be ruthless, though. He's never hurt me like this, before, but he was really angry. I thought he trusted me…" Again, Jackie choked up a bit, then waved her hand in front of Elu and blew her nose once more, and continued: "He believed I was "collaborating with the enemy". Now that Tommy and Leah are gone, I'm sure he'll blame the Brotherhood. He'll figure we're all dead, or no longer worth saving. He'll want to attack them, you know, get revenge. It never takes much to get us to attack each other, but this…this will really drive him crazy."

"You love him, don't you, Jackie?" Elu asked.

There was a pause, and a few more tears. Then Jackie responded: "I did, you know, I mean, yeah, but lately…he's changed. I don't know, he seems, well, paranoid. He thinks everyone's out to get him, not just the Brotherhood. He thinks he needs to look tough or he'll get taken out by his own men and replaced. I mean, we've had our arguments, you know. But, he never hurt me…much, at least. He would say nasty things, and he would threaten me, and…he slapped me a few times, but this…and HE didn't really do it, you know. He sent his guys to do it. He couldn't even look me in the eye and do it…"

At this point, Jackie was unable to continue. She kept looking over at her kids, especially Tommy, the oldest. She kept her voice down, so he couldn't hear her, but Elu could tell he was listening.

"Your kids love their father, too."

"They look up to him. But, now, things are different. Now they know he lied to them. I don't know, I'm not sure Leah gets it, but Tommy does."

"Is there any way we can stop the attack? What would convince them not to? You know that a lot of innocent people will get hurt if we don't. I know you, and Deiondre, wouldn't want that. You're both good mothers."

Jackie swallowed hard and then said: "The only way would be for me or the kids to show up and tell them it wasn't the Brotherhood. But, I'm not going back there, again. I can't!"

"No, no, of course not! It's not safe."

"I can, mom!" It was Tommy. He had stopped pretending to play with the other two kids. He came running up to Elu.

"I can go and tell them. I don't want any more people hurt!"

"No, Tommy, you can't do that. It's too dangerous!" Jackie cried out. As she said that, she leaned forward and grabbed her son, hugging him close.

"I won't put either of you in danger, I promise," said Elu, "but, listen to me. I have a way to get either one of you back into Brigade territory, face to face with Jim Crow, without any danger to either of you. I will not do it unless you're completely OK with it and if you trust me."

"He can, mom, I saw it. When Bishop Elu and Brother Leo came to get us, dad was there. He didn't see anything, even though he was right there. He was froze! All the other kids were froze, too! I don't know how, but they came and got us and nobody knew it until we were gone."

"What? What are you talking about, Tommy?"

"It's true, Jackie. I can walk right through their area, right under their noses, and they can't see me, or anyone I'm with, unless I want them to. I can take their weapons without them even knowing I'm doing it. Do you remember that day at the friary? You and Deiondre were just about to start a fight, and suddenly you were separated? Leo and I had you on opposite sides of the room in a blink, do you remember?"

"Yes…now that I think about it, it was…strange. One moment I was just about to launch into that b…" Jackie caught herself "…I mean, Deiondre, and the next moment I was all the way across the room! What was that?"

"That's the "thing" I can do. It's a talent I've developed, and it can protect all of us, if we're careful."

Jackie sat and thought for a few minutes. Then, she looked Elu in the eye, and said: "Then I'll go! I have some things I need to say to that man, anyway. If you can protect me, I'll go. In fact, if it's OK, Tommy and I will go together. Is that OK, Tommy?"

"I sure will! Let's go!" Tommy started out the door, but Elu grabbed him quickly.

"Good, good, but not quite so fast, Tommy! We need to wait for the signal from Brother Leo. He's checking things out for us. It'll be soon, I'm sure."

Chapter 25

The next morning, very early, Brother Leo returned, as Elu had been expecting. Elu had not yet even gone to the cathedral for morning Mass when he heard a frantic knocking at the door. When he opened it, Leo burst in.

"Bishop, we must hurry! The Brigade is gathering right now at the foot of the bridge, and they plan to march right into the Brotherhood stronghold!"

Elu was prepared for this. He quickly took Leo into intra-time with him, which meant they actually had all the "time" they needed.

"Leo, don't panic. We've got this! We have to go get Jackie and Tommy."

"Jackie and Tommy? What for?"

"They're coming with us."

"Excellency, they can't! It's too dangerous!"

"Yes, it's dangerous, but we can control it. Besides, this is the opportunity we were waiting for! Come on, let's go. They are expecting us."

Elu hurried down the ramp to the next level with Leo trailing after him. They soon arrived at the small apartment and knocked on the door. There was no answer. Then Elu remembered they were in the time gap. He reminded himself to calm down some. He better not make a mistake like that when they confronted Jim Crow!

Elu gently let himself and Leo back into regular time, and again knocked on the door. Very soon, Jackie was there.

"It's time, Jackie. Are you and Tommy ready?"

"Yes, one moment, bishop," Jackie replied. "Tommy, come on. Don't wake your sister. She'll be fine."

As Tommy came into view, Elu took them all into the time gap, and now, again, he knew they were not in a rush.

"Now, Jackie, and Tommy, again I want to be sure you're both OK with this. It's potentially dangerous, even though we have a way to protect you. Are you sure?"

"There's no other way, bishop. And, Tommy and I talked all night about it. He's ready, too."

Tommy nodded. He had a rather grim look on his face, for such a young boy. Elu was convinced.

"OK, then, off we go. Leo will lead us there."

The small group hurried back up the ramp and to the stairway. They ascended the stairs rather quickly, and Leo didn't hesitate to hustle his way towards the lake. He and Tommy led the troop, with Jackie close behind. Elu had some trouble keeping up with them. Finally, they arrived at the bridge.

In the distance, across the river, they could see a large group of people. Elu couldn't make them out very well, but Jackie could.

"That's JCR, and he's leading the entire Brigade! They look like they have all their weapons ready. It's gonna be a massacre!"

"Do they even know where they're going?" asked Elu.

"Oh, sure," Jackie exclaimed. "We have spies and they have spies. The Brotherhood moves around from place to place, just like we do, but we always know where each other is. That also probably means the Brotherhood knows we're coming."

It crossed Elu's mind to ask how they could have effective spies when the groups were so small, but he decided that was for a later discussion.

"They just seem to be standing there," Jackie said. "I don't know what they're waiting for."

Elu smiled. "Well, remember what I told you. They're currently frozen. They'll stay that way as long as we want them to.

We can cross the bridge and approach them without any risk."

Jackie was learning to trust Elu, and understood some of what he had told her the previous night, but she was still skeptical. Elu could see her hesitation, so he took the first step.

"Come on, you all get behind me." He said, as he stepped onto the bridge.

Even with the time gap protection, Elu was being cautious. He walked slowly. Partly he wanted to respect Jackie's trepidation, but he also wanted to be sure he didn't lose his concentration or have something else happen he might not have considered or been prepared for.

Soon, however, they were across the bridge, and face to face with the Brigade and its leaders. Jackie walked very carefully up and stood directly in front of JCR. He didn't flinch and wasn't even breathing, she could tell. He had his old hunting knife in his left hand, and a pistol in the right.

"This is serious, bishop. They don't use the pistols very often. The ammo is scarce, you know, so they try not to waste it. He's really out to get those guys this time."

Elu stepped up to look. Then, he simply reached out and took the knife and the pistol out of Jim Crow's hands. Jackie's eyes got very big watching that. It finally convinced her that Elu was telling the truth. She knew her husband and he would never willing surrender his weapons like that.

"Jackie, step back a bit." Elu said.

Jackie stepped back, and Elu took up a position midway between her and JCR, just off to the side a bit. There was enough space that Elu was certain he could stop things before anything bad happened.

"OK, Jackie, here we go. I'm going to "unfreeze" your husband, but only him. I can freeze him again whenever we need to and I will if he tries anything. Are you ready"?

"Yes, bishop, go ahead." Jackie replied. She was standing there with Tommy up by her side, now, and her left arm around his shoulders.

Elu took a deep breath, and allowed Jim Crow into the time gap.

"What! What's going on!" Jim Crow shouted. He stood there agape, staring at his wife and son, and glancing back and forth to Elu and Leo, also. He rubbed his eyes and then said: "Churchy, are you seeing this?"

Churchy, the second in command, was just behind JCR to his right, and, of course, he just stood there staring blankly and not moving.

"Churchy!" he shouted. He looked over at his sidekick, and gave him a shove. The man simply stood there. JCR looked around behind him, and his entire Brigade seemed rooted to the ground. No one was moving, or talking, or doing anything. Then, he turned back to look at the four figures in front of him.

"What is this? Am I dead? Is this some kind of mirage? Some kind of magic?"

"No, Jimmy," answered Jackie, "it's not a mirage. We're really here."

This was a bit much for JCR to take. There seemed to be a bit of a standoff, and Elu wanted to wait to see how it played out.

Then, Tommy suddenly broke away from his mom. He ran over to his father, and hugged him. Then, he broke away from that embrace, backed up a bit, and kicked Jim Crow in the shin.

"Ow, what was that for?" his father roared.

"You lied to us! You told us the Brotherhood, and Brother Leo, had kidnapped and killed mom! That was all a lie! And, you beat mom up! Why'd you do that?"

The boy was jumping up and down, and obviously quite

angry at JCR. He stopped jumping and moved to kick him again, but Elu caught him.

"I think your father got the message with that first kick, Tommy. Let's let him answer your questions."

"You have no right to question me, boy!" JCR shouted. "I..."

Jackie cut him off. She stepped right up into his face, and said: "Maybe not, but I do! Answer the questions if you're man enough!"

This startled Jim. He had never allowed anyone to speak back to him, and Jackie never had, at least not this boldly. She was finding her courage, though, with the knowledge that Elu was "in charge of things". Elu, on the other hand, was a bit nervous about this confrontation. Their noses were almost touching. If Jim Crow tried something, Elu might not have time to stop it. He started to drop JCR out of the time gap, but before he could, JCR dropped to his knees. Elu backed off and waited.

Jim Crow knelt there for a few moments, his head down. Then he looked up at his wife.

"I'm sorry for hurting you, Jackie. I've never done that before and I never will again! Please, can you forgive me?"

Elu interjected: "Be very careful, Jackie. This is how most abusers will act."

"Who are you, old man? I'm talking to my wife. Back off!" JCR yelled at Elu.

That broke the spell. Jackie knew in her heart that Elu was right. JCR had never beaten her badly, and he hadn't this time, either. This time he had his underlings do it, but he had abused her and the children in many other ways over the years. She knew he wouldn't really change.

"Answer the boy's questions, Jimmy! I don't care if you answer them on your knees, or standing in the lake! Just answer them!"

Jim got up from his kneeling position. His "tears" suddenly seemed to dry up.

"When you disappeared, I assumed you had been captured by those <expletives> across the river. What else was I supposed to think?"

"Don't give me that! You saw me run to Brother Leo's, I know that. You don't have lookouts for nothing!"

"OK, we saw that, but we also saw you and him running south. Where else would you go?"

"So, you figured they killed me, huh?"

"Well, that's what I woulda done!"

"Yeah, so explain to the boy why you had me beat up? Can you explain that away?"

"You were betraying us! You met with that man's woman! We saw that, too, you know."

"And you figured I'd give you up, AND my own kids? You don't trust anybody, do you, Jimmy?"

About this time, Tommy, who had been listening to it all, walked up to his father. Jim Crow bent down, expecting another hug. Instead, the little guy suddenly hauled off and slugged his father right in the nose! Jim staggered a bit, then caught himself. He brought his right arm up to threaten his son, and it was then that he realized he was no longer armed.

"What!? Where's my pistol? Where's my knife? What's going on here??"

Elu, who was now standing a bit away, held up the two weapons. He waved them a bit to be sure JCR saw them, and then he tossed both of them into the river. JCR was enraged, and he abruptly turned and rushed at Elu. Elu, expecting it, pulled JCR out of the time gap. As he froze, Elu simply walked away. Then, he let the man back into intra-time. It was so abrupt that Jim Crow had no time to react and change his momentum. He ended up in the river, also!

Jackie and Tommy laughed out loud, as Elu and Leo smirked quietly. JCR surfaced to hear all that reaction, and climbed out of the river with a grim look on his face. Elu then moved to confront him.

"Mr. Robinson, I'm Bishop Elu. We have been caring for your family in our secret dwelling. I think they have had enough of you. As you can see, it was fairly easy for me to disarm you. I will go around and disarm your entire Brigade. You had better stand down from this attack."

JCR lowered his head, not in any mock atonement, but the way a bull would just before he charged. He looked at Elu angrily. He snorted a few times, but he wasn't in any mood to be humiliated again, so he wasn't about to charge him.

Elu spoke again, this time, in a softer voice.

"I know this has been a difficult confrontation. But, think about it. You are an intelligent man, a leader of men. This war you have been fighting is pointless. You simply kill and your people get killed. It's gone on for too long. If you're a true leader, you'll recognize the benefits of ending it. You can make an agreement with the Brotherhood for no more of it. I can help. You only have to ask."

"I don't need your help, old man," JCR growled.

"Well, take time to think about it, think it through, and, when you're ready, I'll be ready. In the meantime, we're taking your family back to safety."

Elu let JCR think about that for a few moments. Then, he expelled the man from the time gap. Then he led Leo, Jackie and Tommy among the Brigade men. They removed all the weapons they could find, and dumped them also into the river. Then, they made their way back to the tunnels. They had done their best to avoid disaster that day, and Elu hoped it had started something new.

Chapter 26

Jim Crow suddenly stopped and looked around. He looked as if he had seen a ghost. He slowly turned and stared at Churchy.

"What is it, JC?" Churchy asked.

Crow hesitated a moment. He looked around at the rest of the Brigade. Then he said, in low voice: "Churchy, where are your weapons?"

It was only then that Churchy and the rest of them realized they were all empty-handed. Their knives, and spears, and pistols were all missing. Everyone started looking around.

"What the hell?"

"What's going on, here?"

Mostly, however, they were all speechless. Nobody knew what to think.

"Stand down, you guys," shouted JCR. "We can't attack anybody without weapons. We have to go back and re-arm."

"But, JC," Churchy said, "we took all our stuff. We don't have any more back there! What are we gonna do? What happened, anyway?"

"I don't know, Churchy, but one thing I do know, we'll be slaughtered going at the Brotherhood like this. We gotta retreat, and do it now, before they see us like this!"

The Brigade had never retreated, or so they always told themselves. They prided themselves on that. Sometimes they even called themselves "Marines" after the ancient tale of soldiers who never retreated. But, they all realized something was wrong and they had better beat it.

Back at their headquarters, the leaders got together to discuss what had happened.

"I never seen anything like this! You, Churchy?" one of them asked.

"Naw, me neither. I have no idea what happened. Did we forget 'em? Did we just lose 'em on the way?"

"No way, man! We woulda found 'em by now."

Jim Crow was peculiarly silent through this whole discussion. No one dared ask him why or what was going on. It seemed that, somehow, he knew more than he wanted to say. The rest of that day, everyone was very quiet and sullen. No one had any explanations and they all felt quite vulnerable, having been stripped of all their weaponry. They could make more knives and spears, of course, but that would take time. The firearms were a different thing. They were old of course, but well cared for. They were not replaceable, however. This was a terrible loss, they all thought. No one was sure exactly what had happened, or what they should do about it, now.

Meanwhile, south of the river, the Brotherhood was also holding a summit meeting. They had known of the attack, of course, and their lookouts saw the Brigade stop at the bridge and turn back. It was surreal and they also had no idea how to explain it.

"It was like they suddenly decided not to attack us?" asked Chikae, the leader.

"It was more than that. I was watching them in the binoculars. They were armed to the teeth, just as we expected. Then, all at once, they weren't!"

"What do you mean, Kofi?"

"They had spears and pistols, even a rifle or two, that I could see, and then they didn't. It was like they threw them down and ran away."

"Did they? Can we recover the weapons?"

"That's just it...there aren't any! After they left, we snuck up and looked all around. They didn't leave them behind, but they didn't take them, either."

"OK, Kofi, you're not making any sense, here!" exclaimed Dikembe. He was second in command of the Brotherhood, and was known to have a rather short temper. Kofi, one of the scouts, was always quite intimidated by him, even more than he was by Chikae, sometimes.

"Give the kid a break, Dikembe," interjected Deiondre. Unlike the Brigade, the women in the Brotherhood were given more respect and a place in the leadership council. "He can only tell you what he saw. It's our job to interpret it, not his."

Dikembe backed down and, since Kofi really had nothing else to report, he was excused from the meeting.

"Well, now what?" asked Chikae.

"If they ARE unarmed, now's our chance!" shouted Dikembe. "We can march in there and kill 'em all!"

"IF they are unarmed. How do you know it's not some kind of trick?"

Dikembe had nothing to say to that. He was the one who always simply wanted to charge ahead.

"Deiondre, you're pretty quiet. What are you thinking?" asked Chikae.

"It's odd, but I have this feeling it has something to do with those churchmen," she replied to her husband.

"You mean Leo and that strange bishop guy you met?"

"Yeah. That meeting was very strange. I wonder..."

"Strange, how, exactly?"

"Well, you know how long I was gone, right? But while I was there, it seemed a whole lot longer. And then, remember how I said Jackie Robinson tried to attack me? Well, one second she was practically on top of me, and I was preparing to defend myself, and the next second, she was in a distant corner of the room, and those two guys were standing between us. It was very weird."

"What does that mean?"

"Well, I don't know. It was like Leo and the bishop had cast some kind of "spell" on us, that made us forget or something, or maybe we froze up. I don't know, but it was kinda like this…suddenly the Brigade was disarmed, you know?"

The group sat silent for several minutes, trying to make sense of all of this.

"Well," ventured Chikae, "we do know that Leo took Jackie down to Wacker Drive somewhere, after she had been beaten up, remember? I wonder if that's where the bishop is? I wonder if we should check it out?"

The summit meeting was divided about that. Dikembe just wanted to go attack the Brigade, Deiondre was still thinking about the whole thing. The rest were pretty weirded out by it all, and were inclined to stay hunkered down, in case there was going to be a surprise attack. Finally, Chikae made a decision.

"Well, for now, I think we should just stay where we are, and put out as many lookouts as we can, in all directions. If the Brigade tries to surprise us, we'll see them coming. If that bishop does something, maybe we'll see him coming, too. I don't know what else to do."

With that, the meeting broke up, and lookouts were posted. Everyone was pretty much on edge, though.

Chapter 27

After the meeting, as they ate dinner, Deiondre was unusually quiet. She seemed lost in thought.

"What's up, Dee? You seem preoccupied. You still wondering about that stuff with the Brigade?" asked Chikae.

"Yeah, it's very strange. I agree about being cautious, but I wonder if it would be wise to send out a scout. In fact, since I was at that first meeting with Brother Leo, maybe I should go back there, just see what I can find out."

"It's dangerous. Could be a trap. I wouldn't put anything past those Robinsons. And I never trusted that friar."

"He's harmless, Chikae. Besides, I think he really cares. He's a bit naïve and foolish, but he really wants to try to end the fighting. I think that bishop does, too."

"Well, maybe, but the Brigade probably has them all wrapped up. But, if you want to try, I'm not gonna stop you. If anyone can get up there and find something out, it's you."

"Let me think about it. Maybe early tomorrow I can head up there."

As Deiondre spent the evening thinking through her possible reconnaissance mission, another discussion was occurring in the tunnels.

"So, what's gonna happen, now?" asked Jackie. She and her kids were back at Elu and Matilda's, having dinner and just visiting. That was quickly becoming their habit. Matilda liked the company, and Matthew enjoyed playing with his new friends. Jackie just needed some support.

"I don't know," answered Elu. "It's hard to say. How do you think the factions will respond to what happened today?"

"Well, Jimmy and his crew are gonna stew about it for a

bit, then they're likely to move their headquarters, and try to go into hiding. They'll be worried the Brotherhood will know about it and try to attack them while they're defenseless. For good reason, too!"

"Do you think the Brotherhood knows what we did?"

"I know they were watching. But, they probably think it's a trap of some kind, at least for now. When the Brigade doesn't try a surprise attack in the next couple days, the Brotherhood hot heads will prevail and they'll be out for white blood!"

"Who are the hot heads?" asked Elu, who was beginning to realize that Jackie knew a lot more about the situation than he had thought she did.

"One or two of their leaders are pretty gung-ho and they just jump at anything they can to get at us. Their head man, Chi-kae, is pretty levelheaded, and cautious, but most of the men are just out for blood."

"In the meantime," Elu said, as he thought out loud, "perhaps we should consider "disarming" the Brotherhood like we did the Brigade today. Could that be done, do you think?"

Elu aimed this question at both Jackie and Leo. Leo, who was also getting in the habit of making use of Matilda's hospitality, had been sitting in silence as he listened to the exchange between Jackie and Elu. Now he piped up.

"Well, bishop, we could, but it would require knowing exactly where they are right now, and it would require them having their weapons out. If we just went in there, even if we knew where they were, we wouldn't find many weapons. They hide their cache and only bring them out when needed. They keep some defensive stuff around, but not the main collection. They know there are spies around and they don't want to give away their strengths, and all, you know."

"Yeah, Leo's right," agreed Jackie. "We could do that, but only in the right circumstances. It would help a lot, though, at least in the short term. It's kinda not safe to have an imbalance of power like this."

"Well, let's mull this over," suggested Elu, "and let's all keep our eyes and ears open to see if there's anything we can learn. We can talk more tomorrow."

"So, I thought you had some sort of grand plan, or something." Jackie said.

"Not really. My main goal is to get the leaders of the factions together and talk about how to end the fighting. It's clearly to their advantage to do it, they just have to agree."

"Not gonna happen, I don't think. Not as long as Jimmy's in control. He doesn't like to lose, and anything short of wiping out the Brotherhood is "losing" to him. Even if we take away all their weapons, they'll just get more, at least the easy ones like knives and stuff. It'll take them a while, but they'll re-arm."

"Maybe we can change that," Elu said with a smile. "I wonder, in fact, maybe the women could have a part in all of this."

"What do you mean by that?" Jackie asked.

"Well, usually it's the women who want to end things like this. They get tired of seeing their family and friends killed and hurt, and the mothers want to protect their children. The real issue is whether the men will listen to them."

"You can count me out on that one. Jimmy never listened to me, anyway, and the rest of the women, at least in the Brigade, are afraid of their men. You saw what happened to me, and all I did was go to a meeting!"

"You're a strong woman, Jackie. That was clear on the bridge today. Surely, you aren't the only one. There must be more, and I would bet it wouldn't take much to stir them into action, if we could get to them."

"I think that's a bit naïve, bishop. You don't know what it's like up there."

"Well, that's true. On the other hand, we shouldn't sell them short. I suspect they are more courageous than that, especially when it's the safety and well-being of their children at stake."

"Maybe, I don't know."

"Why don't you think about it for a while, and let me know if you have any ideas. See if you can think of anyone that might be willing to run a risk to change things, and how we might get to them."

"OK, I'll think about it, but don't expect much."

Now, as the meal was over, and it was getting a bit late, Leo had to leave to get back to the friary. He promised to be back the next day, to meet a few more of the families. He and Elu were still making the rounds and Leo was becoming well known in the tunnels. They had even had a brief visit with Jennilu, which went better than Elu had hoped for. At least for now she was not fighting against his plans.

Chapter 28

"Brother Leo, you in there?" Called Deiondre. She had risen before sunup, and made her way up to the friary. Now she was standing at the foot of the stairs leading to Leo's front door. He didn't really have a "door" but he did often put a table up on end just to cover the opening at night.

The "door" opened, and Leo peaked out.

"Deiondre! Are you alone?" Leo looked cautiously around and, seeing no one, invited her in.

"Come in, what are you doing here?"

"I think you know, Leo. We saw what happened on the bridge yesterday. I'm pretty sure you know all about it. What exactly was all of that?"

"Let's sit and talk. Would you like some coffee?"

The two of them sat on one of the pews the friars had salvaged many years ago from the wreckage of the church above. They were only about four or five feet wide, and very uncomfortable, but they were the only furniture Leo had, other than a small table and his wooden sleeping rack.

"So, what happened yesterday, Leo? How'd you and the bishop do that?"

"What did you see, Deiondre?"

"You know what we saw. The whole Brigade was about to cross the bridge to attack us. They suddenly turned back and when they did, they were no longer armed. Leo, they were armed to the teeth one minute, and defenseless the next! I was there with the lookouts. Jim Crow had this look of defeat that I've never seen on him before. How'd you do it?"

"Wow, that must have been quite a scene! What makes you think I had anything to do with it?"

"No other explanation, Leo. It was either you or the bishop or both of you. After the encounter we had here, I know you have some way of manipulating things."

"Why do you want to know this, Deiondre? What is the Brotherhood planning?"

"None of your business, friar! But, I can tell you, if it's true, if they are truly dis-armed, there's gonna be a blood bath, and very soon. I don't think you want that."

"What could I possibly do to prevent it? Your leaders have never been in the habit of consulting me about their plans. I'm just a simple friar, you know. Besides, if they are armed or dis-armed, your spies will surely figure that out, and quite quickly, I would think."

Deiondre paused, realizing that she wasn't really getting anywhere. She had come here for a reason, and maybe she should simply come clean about it, she thought.

"What else, Deiondre?" prodded Leo.

Deiondre rose and walked a bit nervously around the small room. She saw Leo's sleeping platform, which still had a few small blood stains on it from Jackie. Leo, of course, had very few resources to clean up such things.

"Is that Jackie's blood there, Leo?" she asked.

Leo looked where she was pointing, but didn't offer anything.

"We saw her, and you helping her, going down State street several days ago. I know she was beaten by that animal she lives with, or by his men."

Leo remained silent. Deiondre turned to face him, and he thought he could see a tear in her eye.

"Leo, I don't want that to be me some day! I don't want anybody to have to endure that anymore! I'm tired of it all. I don't want my kids to have to live with it. It has to stop!"

Leo put his coffee cup down, and simply nodded.

"So, if you know anything, maybe it can help us get out of this terrible situation. You're a man of God, right? You have to help us, Leo!"

Leo rose, and faced Deiondre.

"Yes," he said, "I am a man of God, and, yes, I have to help you. More than that, Deiondre, I WANT to help! I may have a way to do that. It would require you trusting me, and I would have to trust you, that you are not going to simply go to Chikae and Dikembe with this and use it against me or the Brigade."

"How can I get you to trust me, Leo?"

Leo paused for a few moments, then a plan began to form.

"If you will trust me, I will trust you. Stay here in my friary, while I go on an errand. If you are still here when I return, then I will trust you and we can have a discussion. Are you willing to do that?"

"Yes, Leo, I'll wait. How long will you be gone?"

"Not long," Leo replied, and he headed out the door. Deiondre sat back down on the pew to wait.

Leo hustled down the street and soon he was down the stairway and knocking on the bishop's door. It was just early enough that Elu had not yet gone to the cathedral.

"Leo," Elu said as he opened the door, "you are early, my friend." Then, seeing the friar was sweaty and out of breath, he added, "what is it, Leo? What's going on?"

Leo came in and they sat on the sofa.

"Deiondre is waiting for me back at the friary, bishop! She arrived very early this morning. She was sent, I think, to find out what happened at the bridge, and she knows it involved us. But, she is asking for help to stop all the violence."

Elu raised his eyebrows and was briefly speechless. Leo

went on and explained the whole conversation.

"And so, bishop," he concluded, "I decided to come here and see what you would suggest. I don't think it's safe to bring her here, but perhaps you could return with me and the three of us could talk. Do you think Jackie should come, also?"

Elu thought for a moment. He had already taken the precaution of slipping the two of them into intra-time to have their discussion. He just had a premonition that it would be a good idea.

"Leo, this is another "opportunity", I think. I'll come with you. I think for now we should leave Jackie here. I don't want to stir up anything. Deiondre might be more forthcoming with just the two of us. What do you think?"

"Yes, I would agree, bishop. If she's still waiting when we get there, I hope we can begin to move on this."

Elu finished getting ready very quickly and the two of them hastened out of the dwelling and up the stairway to meet Deiondre.

Chapter 29

Using the time gap, Elu and Leo still hurried up the street. They were both anxious to see what Deiondre would want to do. They flew down the stairs at the friary and found themselves both sweaty and out of breath. Elu decided they should recover a bit before they brought Deiondre into intra-time with them. After a few minutes of rest, they were feeling back to normal.

"Well, we aren't as young as we thought we were, anymore, huh, Brother Leo?" asked Elu.

Leo smiled and agreed with the bishop.

"Ok, I think we're OK now, let's see what Deiondre has to tell us."

They both went back out of the room briefly so as not to startle the woman by simply "appearing" out of thin air in front of her. Then Elu allowed her into the time gap and they knocked and entered the room.

Deiondre stood up when she saw them.

"You two are like cats! I never even heard you coming!"

"Good morning, Deiondre," exclaimed the bishop. "It's so good to see you again. Leo says you have lots of questions and I hope we can help."

The three sat down again on the available small pews. Deiondre hesitated a moment, then began.

"Bishop, please don't bother to deny you had anything to do with the events on the bridge yesterday. I know better. I don't know how you did it, but it's done and I have more serious concerns."

Elu nodded and motioned for her to go on.

"As I told Leo, I saw what they did to Jackie. I...hope she's OK. She and I don't agree on much. We've only met a few times, but one thing I think she and I would probably both want, is for no one else to have to suffer like that. Frankly, I'm tired of all the fighting and violence, all the killing. I want my kids to have a normal life, whatever that is..."

"I understand," said Elu. Then he simply waited for her to go on.

"There are rumors that you have a whole group of families down in the tunnels, someplace. Do they have normal lives? Do they fight like we do?"

"No, they don't fight, Deiondre. In fact, they all work together. They go to church together and their kids go to school together. Is that what you want?"

Deiondre had to fight back some tears. It took her a moment to get herself back together.

"I'd give anything for my two kids to go to school, you know, like normal kids used to."

"We have quite a number of children the same ages as yours. I'm sure they would get along quite well."

"Do they all...well...look like you? You know, we've been fighting over the color of people's faces for so long, it might take them a while, but if they are sorta brown, like you two, it would go easier."

Elu laughed out loud. "Yes, Deiondre, they all pretty much look like me. I have to confess, we don't focus too much on that, but maybe it's because we all look the same. When we entered the tunnels, several generations ago, we were black and white and Asian and Native American, and we all "blended" eventually! We all get along very well, just as our ancestors did...just as you and the Brigade could someday!"

Deiondre smiled a bit, through her tears, then she got down to practical issues.

"Bishop, if the Brigade has really been disarmed, and if the

Brotherhood finds out, there's going to be a vicious attack! Many will die. I'm not sure how to prevent that. But, if we could, somehow, this might be a starting point for something better."

"I agree, Deiondre. I'm not usually in favor of forcing people into something, but we have sort of done that with the Brigade, haven't we? If we could somehow disarm the Brotherhood, too, then the playing field would be level and perhaps cooler heads could prevail. What do you think?"

"It could work, but then there're the ones who always want to fight. They'll fight with their fists if they have nothing else."

"What do the other women think, Deiondre? Do any of them share your concerns?"

"It's hard to say, bishop, because no one talks about things like that out in the open. I've heard some things, though. Of course, because I'm part of the leadership council and married to the leader, they're a bit reluctant to tell me things like that."

"What's your gut tell you, Deiondre? If we disarmed the Brotherhood and then made an announcement about it, with, perhaps, you doing it, do you think many of the women would join a "peace movement"?"

Deiondre thought about that for a moment.

"It would be risky, but, it might work. It's probably less risky than not doing anything, though. The stakes are high, bishop, but the potential reward is much higher!"

"Then, let me ask you one other thing…Jackie has recovered from her injuries. She and her children are with us in the tunnels. She feels the same way you do. What if the two of you joined hands, and made this declaration together? Do you think that would work?"

This idea made Deiondre's head swirl! It was totally contrary to everything she had been taught and how she and her people had lived for centuries. It took her a while to process the whole thing.

"Would she be willing?" she finally asked Elu.

"I think she would. I have not specifically brought it up to her, yet, but I believe so."

"If she would, I'd do it, bishop. This whole thing has to stop!"

"Deiondre, thank you for being so honest and open with us! What do you see as the first step?"

"The first thing we have to do is dis-arm the Brotherhood. But, they can't see us doing it! They can't see ME doing it, for sure! I'll end up just like Jackie, probably worse! And, my kids and I would need protection of some kind, until this whole thing is over."

"We can do that, Deiondre. I can promise it!"

The three of them then plotted out the practical issues, and were soon ready to go.

Chapter 30

Still under cover of the time gap, Elu, Leo, and Deiondre made their way south to Brotherhood territory. She led them right into the heart of the group's headquarters. Most of the men were there, preparing for the usual morning gathering. They met every day to consider the previous day's events and prepare for any upcoming assaults.

"That's Chikae, over there, leaning against the wall," Leo said to Elu. He pointed him out. "And, next to him is Dikembe. They are the first and second in command."

"That's right," replied Deiondre. "And Dikembe is the real hot-head! He'd kill any white man on sight. In fact, it's rumored that he has."

"What should we do?" asked Elu.

"Well, they'll all have their pieces and knives on them. We can get those easy enough, and dump them in this bin, then take them out to the river. There's a small cache of similar weapons behind that door, but there's another larger one nearby. They should all fit in this bin."

Deiondre had picked up a large empty trash bin. She and the two churchmen went around the room, picking up weapons as they went. They were able to get everything from the two caches, also.

"Is that it, then?" asked Elu.

"Not quite. There are the men out on lookout duty, and a couple that simply aren't here at the moment. I know where to find all of them. It should be fairly easy. There is one other more difficult issue."

"What is it?"

"There's a large store of explosives we have to get rid of.

It's too much to carry away, and some of them are rather heavy. It would be best to blow it all up, but that could be an issue. It's close by and it would be a large explosion."

"Let's get rid of all of these, first, then we can go look at the storeroom." Elu offered.

The three of them took a while dragging the full bin to the river and dumping everything. Then, they replaced the bin and went searching for the storeroom. With Deiondre's help, it wasn't hard to find. The room was huge and it was packed with explosives.

"Wow!" exclaimed Elu. "This would level several blocks! We can't just explode it here – at least, not with all these people around. What can we do?"

After scoping out the area, they agreed to not deal with it just yet. Such an effort really required more thought and planning, so they left it as it was and headed toward the stairway.

"Deiondre, you have trusted us, so now I'm going to trust you. I am going to let you into our tunnel area. Would you want us to bring your children along with us?" Elu said.

Deiondre thought about it for a moment, then decided to go alone.

"I want to see it first. I want to be able to tell my kids that I know it's safe because I've been there, first. They're safe where they are for now."

And so, the three of them descended the stairs down to the tunnels. It was only as they were standing at Elu's doorway that he allowed them all to leave intra-time.

"Wait here a moment. Let me prepare my wife for this meeting. I don't want to startle her!" Elu said. His real motive, however, included Jackie. If she was there, having her and Deiondre come abruptly face to face might not be very wise. He left the other two on the landing, and went into the dwelling. As expected, there was Jackie, sitting and talking to Matilda. She must have arrived almost immediately after Leo and I left, Elu thought. They had been "frozen" there ever since. He was glad he had been cautious. He closed the door behind him.

"Oh, Elu, have you been at Mass already?" Matilda asked, as Elu entered.

"Oh, well, not really. I have something to tell both of you. But first, I have someone you both need to meet. Please be calm. There is nothing to fear. Everything's under control!" He looked right at Jackie as he spoke. Then, Elu turned and opened the door, inviting the others in.

Leo came in, followed by Deiondre. She had been warned by Leo, before Elu opened the door, that Jackie might be there, visiting with Matilda. As she entered, Jackie jumped up from the sofa and stood there, poised, as if she were ready to run. The two surface women eyed one another up and down for several moments.

"I'm glad to see you are well, Jackie. I was worried about you. We saw how badly they had hurt you," Deiondre offered.

"Your people have done as much," Jackie responded.

"Yes, and I think it's time it all stopped. What do you think?"

Jackie hesitated for a moment, then nodded.

"I agree. No one else should suffer as we have. I...I'm sorry, Deiondre, for...all the pain our people have given you."

"And I'm sorry, too..."

With that, the two women spontaneously embraced and cried on one another's shoulders. The others in the room simply stood there, allowing them to express their pain together.

After several minutes, Elu spoke up.

"Well, it's getting late in the morning, and I haven't eaten yet. Anyone up for breakfast?"

Matilda grinned and hustled into the kitchen, which was really just a few steps away, and began working up a meal. Elu offered everyone chairs around their small table, and poured some coffee.

"We have a lot to discuss, but first, we need to eat!" he exclaimed.

As they began the meal, Elu paused to say the meal prayer. Matilda and Leo bowed their heads, as did Matthew who had just joined them. Jackie was starting to get used to this, so she bowed a bit hesitantly, but Deiondre was taken by surprise. Realizing she should have expected this, though, she quickly joined the others and bowed her head for the momentary prayer.

As they passed around the platters, Elu started up a discussion.

"So, Jackie, how are the kids adjusting? Have they been to the classroom, yet?"

"Yes, bishop, they were there yesterday afternoon. Matthew was very nice and helped them get acquainted with everyone. They really like Miss Theresa."

"Miss Theresa is our teacher," Elu explained to Deiondre. "She teaches all the grades, and everyone's there all at once. It's not a large group."

"Yes it is, Elu," corrected Matilda. "Remember, you only visit them in the morning. Actually, she teaches the younger kids in the morning and the older ones in the afternoon. There are probably a couple dozen or more in each session."

"Oh, you're right, Mattie. I forgot. The older ones come to the cathedral for their session. Well, that happens when you get older! Forgetting, I mean, not going to the cathedral!"

"How is the apartment, dear?" asked Matilda.

"It's really great, actually. Much better than anything I've ever had before. The kids love it. I took your advice, too. I hung up some of the pictures you gave me. It's starting to feel like home, and it's only been a few days."

"Where do you live, now?" asked Deiondre. She was getting very interested in the conversation.

"The bishop and Mattie set us up in a spare apartment on the second level. It's right down from the school. It's not as large as this one, of course, but it's really nice. Much better than an old bombed out skyscraper lobby!"

"I know how those are!" exclaimed Deiondre. "Could I maybe see it, later?"

"Sure, we can give you a tour, if that's OK with bishop." Jackie replied.

"I think it's a splendid idea!" Elu commented. "We should do that before we talk strategy or anything."

Jackie had not been part of the previous discussions with Deiondre, but this mention of strategy didn't faze her. She had a pretty good idea why Elu had brought her former nemesis into the tunnels.

Soon breakfast was over, and Leo volunteered to help Matilda with cleaning up, to free up the other ladies, who wanted to help some.

"No, no, I'm used to this. This is what a friar is for, to serve, you know. You go on your tour," he said.

Elu and the two women left and took Matthew with them. Their first stop was Jackie's apartment. Jackie knocked on the door, just to warn her kids that she was coming in.

"Are you two up, yet? It's almost time for school. Matthew is here to go with you." She cried into the void.

There were the usual groans, and soon two little shadows appeared in the darkness, and two young voices said they were ready to go.

"I had them up earlier. They really were ready to go, I think they went back to sleep," Jackie intoned, as she switched on the small light in the apartment.

Then there was a scream, and both kids ran into the bathroom, the only part of the apartment with a separate door.

"Oops! Deiondre, I apologize! I don't think they were expecting you!"

"My kids would have done the same thing, Jackie. Not a problem. I'd be surprised if they didn't react that way."

"It's OK, you can come out. We're all safe. This is just my friend, Deiondre, and the bishop."

The door opened just a crack. Tommy peered out, and croaked: "Are you sure? Is it a trap?"

"No, silly! Not in the tunnels. Come out of there right now!"

Both of the kids very cautiously came out, and looked at Deiondre, who was smiling at them. The bishop was there and then Matthew came running over.

"Come on, you guys, we're gonna be late for school!"

Soon the young ones were down the hall, and Jackie was showing off her apartment to Deiondre.

"It's not big and it's not much, but it beats the he...oops, sorry bishop. It beats anything upstairs." Jackie said.

"Yes, it's very nice," commented Deiondre. She looked all around and was quite impressed.

"Well, let's see the school and then I'd like to show you our farm." Elu replied.

At the classroom door, Elu motioned to Miss Theresa, who came over to greet the visitors.

"Class," said Miss Theresa, turning toward the children, "we have visitors. Bishop Elu is giving tours. This is Miss Jackie,

Tommy and Leah's mother, and this is Miss Deiondre. She's visiting today, also. Let's all say hello."

All the kids stood and turned toward the door and said in unison: "Good morning, Bishop and Miss Jackie and Miss..." What came out of the collective voices wasn't quite "Deiondre" but it passed as a greeting, at least. Elu greeted the children and then apologized for have to run, but they had a schedule to keep and he didn't want to distract from Miss Theresa's schedule, either. The trio left, then, to go down the ramps to the bottom level.

"Well, bishop, you were telling the truth about the school and this whole place," Deiondre said on their way down the ramp. "I'm very impressed. I'm sure you feel very secure here, Jackie. I'm happy to see that."

Jackie smiled and said she did, and was especially happy for her kids. Elu couldn't hardly repress his smile. This was working, he thought!

<hr>

Chapter 31

<hr>

"Well, let's talk. We have some news for you, Jackie," said Elu as he and the two women took their places around the kitchen table. Matilda served them more coffee, then sat next to Elu.

"What news?" Jackie asked.

"Deiondre, do you want to tell her?"

"We dis-armed the Brotherhood this morning! We found them all and we took all their weapons and dumped them in the river."

Jackie was startled. This was not something she expected, at least not so soon.

"Wow! That means the "balance" is restored. Do they know it?"

"Well, they should by now," explained Elu. "We "froze" them, and took all their weapons, but they have been "unfrozen" since before we began our breakfast! They're probably scurrying around right now, trying to figure out where their guns and knives are!"

"That's true, but it also means I should be getting back there. They were expecting me to go "scouting" for you and Leo but the longer I'm gone, the more suspicious they will be," explained Deiondre.

"Well, here we go...there," said Elu, "we are now in the time gap, and so no more time will elapse for them for the "time" being...so to speak!"

Elu was always amazed at how many time references crept into everyday speech. Each "time" he wanted to say something like he just did, he hesitated, trying to figure out how to talk about time, during intra-time! He usually just gave up and said whatever seemed to make sense to those around him. Of course, the whole thing simply confused everyone else, anyway, so they just let him ramble most of the "time".

"We do have one other problem. The Brotherhood, and I presume the Brigade, also, has a huge stockpile of explosives. Those need to be eliminated, somehow. I'm open to suggestions."

"Yes, bishop," answered Jackie. "The Brigade has a huge cache also. There's more than just explosives, though. There's also the raw materials and the tools they use to make all that stuff. Somehow, we need to get rid of all of that."

This made Elu pause and think. It wouldn't be easy. It was also rather urgent. As soon as the factions realized what was going on, and knew that their explosives were their only recourse, they would start using them. This was also always a difficult topic for him and for Matilda, because it was those explosives that had disrupted their lives so badly just a few years ago. As they sat and talked about it, Elu glanced over at his wife and found her with a tear in her eyes, as she looked over at where Matthew stored his toys. He was always a reminder to her of the loss of Rachel.

"What do you suggest we do?" Elu finally asked.

"There are multiple options, and maybe we need to do a little bit of all of it," commented Jackie.

"What exactly do you mean?"

"Well, we can bury them where they are, we could try somehow to flood the storeroom, or we could explode them. We could also remove some of them and bury them elsewhere, or dump them in the lake or the river. Those choices all have drawbacks," she replied.

"Yeah, we could do any or all of those, but it all depends on timing and knowing exactly where they are, you know. I mean, the surroundings and all the options. It would sure be nice to have some kind of map or something," added Deiondre.

"Maybe we do!" Exclaimed Elu. "Wait here a moment!"

Elu jumped up and ran into his study. They could hear him rummaging around a bit, then he came out with a load of large books. He laid them on the table and pulled one out.

"This may help us!"

As he thumbed through the pages, he realized it was getting very quiet. He looked up and saw quizzical looks on the faces of the two young women.

"Oh! I may have skipped a step! Do you two know much about books and maps and things?" he asked, a bit sheepishly.

"Not really," admitted Jackie.

"No," said Deiondre. "Frankly, I never learned to make much sense out of those things. Reading is not exactly something we do much in the Brotherhood."

"I'm sorry, I assumed too much. Let me see what I can find in here and then we can look at the maps together."

He continued thumbing along until he came up on a particular chart. It was labeled: "Central tunnel system" and dated from before the calamities. The pages were a bit yellowed and fragile, but they were quite legible. This page was a fold out one. Elu spread it over the table, and everyone bent over to look at it.

"OK," he said, "here is the lake, and here is the river. These lines are the tunnels of various kinds. You can see here is the legend. The deeper ones are dashed like this, and certain colors, etc. We are here. The Brotherhood headquarters is…here!"

"That's right!" exclaimed Deiondre, "That's exactly where it is! And, here is where the explosives are stored, in this tunnel, down a few levels."

As they explored the diagram, Jackie suddenly realized something.

"Look, this other tunnel is right alongside where the explosives are, and it runs up, I think, from there, and goes straight out to the lake, almost."

"Yes, it does," agreed Elu.

"If we could get through those walls, say with a small explosion or two, we could flood that whole area!" Deiondre blurted out.

"You're right, I don't think it would take much to blast through those walls."

"So, where is the Brigade's storage?" asked Elu.

They turned their attention to the north side of the river.

"It's sorta like the Brotherhood place," commented Jackie. "We store them in a tunnel, several levels down, to keep them safe. Here! This is the place."

Jackie had her finger on the spot, and everyone began perusing the map. Elu was very enthusiastic about it. He accidentally bumped heads with Jackie.

"Oops, I'm so sorry!"

"Husband, you need to get out of the way! Let the ladies do this, they know what they're doing!" exclaimed Matilda.

Elu blushed a bit, and backed out of the way, realizing his wife was right.

"Here," squealed Deiondre, "this is very much the same! There are tunnels all around it and one leads off to the river, here. We could probably do the same thing!"

Everyone peered at what Deiondre was pointing at, even Elu, being careful not to bump heads again.

"Yes, it certainly appears so. I have a question, though. Are these storehouses in a position where they could drain the water away if we flood them? We would have to be careful about that," he asked.

"Probably not," ventured Jackie. "I know on our side, we tried to position them in the deepest tunnel we could find, in our area, there. There are no other tunnels beneath it, it doesn't look like. I don't think there are any drains or anything, either, as I recall."

"I don't think we have any, either," said Deiondre. "If we flood it, it should stay flooded, both of them, it looks like."

"This is doable, I think, Ladies! We need a plan, now."

"Can't we just do like we did before, "freeze" them all and sneak in and do it?"

"Well, to some extent, but it's a bit more complicated. We can only do one side at a time, and there needs to be a sequence, you know. We need to blow up one and then the other. Also, there is the not-so-small problem that explosions don't work in the time gap," Elu explained.

Everyone else seemed a bit confused, so Elu added: "If we "freeze" everything, we have to "unfreeze" it all, at least temporarily, for the explosives to work. They are frozen like everything else, you see."

The women nodded, although the niceties of time freezing were a bit beyond them. They trusted Elu. He clearly knew what he was doing.

"It also all depends on the tunnel structure still being the same as when this map was made, doesn't it? I mean, over the years, could there have been collapses or other things that might make it not so easy?" asked Jackie.

"Yes, very true. We won't know until we get out there and look!"

With that as a plan, and carrying the maps, the three of them, minus Matilda, left to scout out the situation.

Chapter 32

"So, Deiondre, who are your "friends"?" said the huge black man, who stepped out in front of them on the street. He had emerged from behind a large pile of rubble, and stood there grinning at Elu and Jackie. Deiondre had been following behind them.

Elu was so startled, he nearly passed out! Jackie even had to steady him. He glanced back at Deiondre, and then saw two other black men coming up from behind them. In that same instant, he realized he could hear the sounds of the city, and even saw a bird fly by. This was not supposed to happen! Somehow, he had slipped them all out of intra-time and back into regular space-time. He hurried to readjust, but realized he simply couldn't do it!

The big man was still blocking their way. Then he heard Deiondre.

"I was coming back from my recon when I found these two, snooping around where they shouldn't have been snooping!"

"Well, then," said the big fellow, "maybe they need a little reminder to stay on their side of the river!"

As he said this, he punched his fist into his other open hand, and gave Elu a menacing look.

"Just take it easy, Dikembe, I'm sure Chikae would want to question them. They could answer a whole lot easier if you haven't punched out their teeth!"

Dikembe looked a bit disappointed, but agreed, and so Deiondre and the three black men led Elu and Jackie into a nearby abandoned building. They went down a staircase, into the basement, and soon found themselves in a large, dimly lit area, with a lot of other men and a few women.

"So, Deiondre, where's your weapon?" asked Dikembe.

Deiondre made a show of surprise, and said: "Whoa! It was right here in my hand a moment ago! What happened? Did I drop it?"

The fellows behind her said they hadn't seen anything. Dikembe looked at her a bit strangely, then said: "Well, you know, the same thing happened to all of us, just a while ago. While you were out, suddenly all our weapons disappeared! We've been trying to figure it out. It was like what happened to the Brigade the other day. I bet these two know something about it, right?"

Elu and Jackie found themselves surrounded by at least a dozen threatening faces. Some of the men were making gestures as if they were about to attack. Then, abruptly, everyone froze, except Elu and Jackie.

"Looks like you got yourself in a little too deep, elder!"

Elu spun around and found himself face to face with Adeevan.

"Adeevan! What are you doing here?"

"I could sense you were in danger, elder. Who else should we rescue? Who was with you?"

"Well, let's get Jackie, here. I think Deiondre should stay here with her people for now. Wow, you're just in time, Adeevan! It was getting sticky in here!"

Soon Adeevan, Elu and Jackie were out of the place, and on down the street back to the stairway.

"So, who exactly are you?" asked Jackie.

Adeevan smiled and said: "I think I'll let the elder answer that question, my friend."

"Well," said Elu, "this is my friend, Adeevan. He is the one who taught me about intra-time."

"A little too well, too, it seems! We need to talk about all of this, bishop," Adeevan commented, as they made their way down the stairway. At the bottom, they let Jackie go toward her apartment, but as she left, Elu saw her suddenly "freeze" half-way down the ramp.

"Well, your friend is now out of intra-time, elder and it is only the two of us. Let's sit and talk."

They adjourned to Elu's study. Adeevan sat and Elu paced.

"What happened, Adeevan? We were going along fine and suddenly it seems I lost it!"

"Yes, I know."

"That's another thing. How did you know?"

"Let's just say I keep an eye on my "students". I could tell you were in trouble and it seemed I should show up."

"It's been a while. I thought you had forgotten about me! I was worried you got lost in one of those time streams you told me about!" exclaimed Elu.

"No, no, I haven't. It's certainly possible, and I have had that happen before, but having friends like you helps keep me oriented in the time streams, you know."

"No, not exactly. What do you mean?"

"Well, let's see how I can explain this. I'm sure you must realize that I have other "students" in other places in the time stream. I don't mentor people just to be nice, you know. It helps me, also. The more you use intra-time at your point in space-time, the more, um…dilated…yes, that's the word, the more dilated the time stream becomes at this point. It makes it easier to find. It's like, say, a signpost. I can use the signposts from the various times to keep me oriented and I can more safely navigate the various streams."

Elu basically stared at Adeevan as if he were speaking Greek or something.

"It's a bit complicated, I'm afraid," Adeevan said. "You know, some of the time streams go one way and some go backwards, so it's really important…oh, well, I see it's getting to be a bit technical."

"Um, yeah, I guess that's the word for it...or just...I don't know, I have basically no idea what you just said..."

"Well, that's not why I'm here. I said we need to talk. There are some things you need to understand, elder. You've been using intra-time an awfully lot lately. You do need to be careful."

"Careful? What do you mean, exactly?"

"Well, one problem is what you experienced today. If you are using intra-time a lot, frankly you get exhausted! You can't keep it up for so long. You need to rest a bit more between episodes, you see. Right now, I'd say you need to spend at least a day out of it."

"So, rest between episodes."

"Yes, and not so many episodes each day, either."

"If I rest enough, then, I could go a bit longer for something special?"

"You could, but you still need to be careful. If you're using intra-time a lot, it gets, well, "normal" to you. You start to prefer intra-time, and you may get to where you can't really tell the difference. You can get stuck in it! You can get...dependent, I guess, on it."

"Oh! That could be a problem!"

"Yes, it can be very difficult. You could end up like me, elder. You don't want that to happen."

"What do you mean, exactly?"

"Well, that's a topic for another time, I think. For now, just rest today, and be a bit more careful with it after that. I'll keep an eye out for you, but I'm not always immediately available to rescue you, so just...be cautious."

"Thank you, Adeevan, I will. Would you like to meet my

wife? She's been asking about you…"

Suddenly, Elu was alone again, and he could hear sounds coming from the rest of the dwelling. He realized he was back in regular space-time, and decided it was a good time for a nap! He was exhausted!

Chapter 33

"Elu, dear, it's time for dinner!"

Elu shook himself awake, and glanced over at the big hourglass. He had slept for several hours! He got up and tottered from his study to the kitchen table. Matilda and Matthew were already there.

"Where's Jackie? She and the kids are usually here," asked Elu.

"She was here, but she left. She was very worried about you, Elu. She didn't want to disturb your rest, but she does want to talk to you sometime after dinner. I said I'd have you come down to her apartment."

"That's good, thank you. Wow, I really did sleep for quite a while, didn't I?"

"You were obviously exhausted. What happened up there? Jackie was a bit closed about it, but mentioned that young man of yours, what's his name?"

"Oh, Adeevan! Yes, it was quite remarkable. He simply appeared when we needed him most! I tried to get him to stay and meet you, but he just disappeared, again!"

"Well, I'm glad Jackie saw him. I was beginning to think you had imagined him!"

Elu chuckled to himself, but then remembered Adeevan's warning. He began to wonder if some of this intra-time stuff was starting to get to him. After dinner, he walked down the ramp to visit Jackie and the kids. He knocked and Leah answered the door.

"You kids can play without me. I'm going with the bishop for a talk, OK?" said her mom.

Jackie came out into the tunnel and closed the door.

"I don't really want them hearing a lot of this, you know. I'm afraid they'll worry, or just get too nosy about things they don't need to know about, you understand, bishop."

"Yes, I do, Jackie. That's a wise precaution."

"Where can we go to talk?"

"Well, we could always go up to the sundial. That's a nice place to sit, sometimes. There is still enough light for now, but there shouldn't be anyone around to bother us."

The two made their way back up the ramp, and then across to the middle of that upper level. They sat on some old metal benches that had been set up many years ago around the edge of the old sundial.

"So, bishop, what exactly happened today?"

"Well, Adeevan says I was simply exhausted from holding us all in the time gap for so long and for so many "adventures" over a short period of time. It was very weird! I was unable to concentrate enough to get us back into it. It was fortunate that Adeevan showed up when he did!"

"So, OK, who's this Adeevan fellow, anyway? He seemed very mysterious and strange!"

"Well, I don't frankly know his whole story. He is the one who has been mentoring me with this intra-time thing. I think there's more to him than we realize. In the meantime, though, we have more pressing things to consider."

"Yes, we do! What do you think has happened with Deiondre? Was it wise to leave her back there at the Brotherhood?"

"I think we had to. They saw her. They expected her back from her reconnaissance mission. She did a good job suddenly coming up with that line about finding us snooping around, and I bet she can hold her own. But, I do think we need to reconnect with her very soon. We don't want to lose our momentum."

"What should we do?"

"I'd like to go meet her briefly tomorrow, but then spend the rest of the day away from the time gap. We can instead spend our time looking over the maps and making some plans. I'm mainly concerned that we need more expertise for this effort than just you and I and Deiondre have."

"What do you think we need?"

"Well, it would be really great to have an engineer and an explosives expert, but I simply don't know any, at least not in the tunnels. We do have someone very familiar with things like pipes and flowing water, and things. I think you met him, Richard LH. He heads our water crew and he might know enough to help us with that part. Do you know anyone you could trust from the Brigade to help us with the explosives?"

"Not that I could trust, no, but let me think about it."

"Well, I'll ask Deiondre, too, tomorrow. Why don't we plan to meet tomorrow, say mid-morning, and go over the charts, and things? I'll try to visit Deiondre sometime before that."

They agreed on the plan and Elu went back home for an early bedtime. He was still quite tired. "This time stuff really wears you out," he thought to himself.

The next morning, after early morning Mass, Elu started up the stairway. He got about halfway up, before he dared to try entering intra-time again. It actually went rather smoothly. He got up to the surface, and looked around from under the canopy. Things were silent. The river was not moving. There were no birds flying around. He "felt" like he was in the time gap. He cautiously ventured out into the open and began to walk carefully toward the lake. Soon, he found the place they had been taken the day before.

There was no one around, and so Elu tiptoed into the building, and down the short stair way. He found himself back in the Brotherhood headquarters again. There were quite a few people standing around. No one was moving. Elu took a breath, realizing he had been holding it in all the way down the stairs. He slinked around the room, between people and piles of various equipment and debris. Suddenly, he saw Deiondre. She was sitting in a circle of several others. Elu recognized Dikembe from yesterday.

He inched his way up to beside Deiondre. Then he realized he shouldn't suddenly appear in front of her. It would probably scare her half to death! He walked around the group, and positioned himself a bit behind the man directly opposite her. He then brought her into intra-time with him.

"Oh!" Deiondre exclaimed. Then she covered her mouth, and looked around. Everyone else seemed "frozen". She partially whispered to Elu: "Is it safe?"

Elu nodded, and told her: "Yes, it's fine. I have it under control now. Can we talk?"

Deiondre got up from her chair and motioned for Elu to follow her. They went into an adjacent room, small and rather dark.

"Are you alright? What happened yesterday? Suddenly we were in normal time, I guess, and then suddenly you and Jackie were gone! What's going on?"

"I am so sorry, Deiondre! I put you in a very difficult position! It's bothered me ever since. We are fine, but how are you?"

"I'm good. They bought my story. They had no reason not to. There have been very strange things going on but nobody believes I could have had anything to do with it, although Dikembe did give me a strange look right after you guys disappeared."

"I'm so happy to hear. Jackie was worried about you, too! So, the short answer is, I had been doing too much of the time gap stuff and it simply wore me out! I have a mentor, who has been teaching me these techniques. He showed up just in time and basically took Jackie and I away and back to the tunnels. He made me rest all day yesterday!"

"I'm sure it must be exhausting, although I have no idea how any of this works."

"Well, the problem is, it's exhausting but in a stealthy sort of way! As far as I can tell, it exhausts me without me realizing it! I'm going to have to be more careful. I don't want a repeat of what happened yesterday."

"So, what's our plan? I presume we're still going on with things."

"Yes, I think we should. But I need to be respectful of your feelings, Deiondre. Jackie wants to go ahead. Are you OK with it, still?"

"Yes, bishop, I am. Yesterday just reinforced it to me. Those guys were ready to beat you and Jackie something terrible! And I'm sure they would have done even worse things to her. We need to end this cycle of violence!"

"Jackie and I plan to spend the day going over the charts and maps. I'm going to try to enlist one of our men who has experience in what you might call "water dynamics". One thing we're missing, though, is someone with some explosives experience. I'm not sure the three of us should try to do that on our own. Jackie's thinking about it, but so far knows no one she could trust from the Brigade."

Deiondre nodded, and was quiet for a moment.

"I might have someone, bishop. But, it could be tricky getting to him. Let me sound him out just a bit, and then I'll have to let you know. When will I hear from you again?"

"Well, probably tomorrow. I still need a bit of rest, but tomorrow we should be good. I'll try to come around the same time, and then we can go do our scouting. Will that work?"

"Sure. I'll be ready."

Deiondre then went to take her place in the discussion

circle once again. Elu dropped her out of the time gap, and returned home.

Chapter 34

"Keontae, do you have a minute?" Deiondre asked her brother. He was one of the advance scouts, and was at the front of just about every action between the Brigade and the Brotherhood. He was heading out for his watch near the Lake Shore Drive bridge.

"Hey, sis, I've been worried about you! I heard you ran into some spies during your recon mission. Sounds like you got the better of them, huh?"

"Yeah, it was more luck than anything. You know how those things go."

"I sure do. What's up?"

"So, I was wondering what you thought about all of this stuff that's been doing on. You were there on watch that day, weren't you, when the Brigade nearly invaded us, right?"

"Yeah, it was the damnedest thing, too! Never seen anything like it. Their weapons just seemed to disappear and they looked like they were just…lost, I guess. Then they retreated. It was really weird, alright!"

"Dikembe wanted us to attack right then, you know. I guess it was lucky we didn't, since we ended up losing our weapons, too," Deiondre commented.

"Of course, Dikembe wanted to attack! He always wants to attack. Doesn't matter to him, he's always looking for a fight. He's gonna get us all killed one day," Keontae replied.

"What do you think?"

"I don't know. We gotta keep our watch up. Could be a trick or something.

"What else?"

"Whatta you mean?"

"Hey, brother to sister, you know, just between us. What else you thinking? What should we really do? I can tell you're thinking about it, Keontae."

"Well…I'm loyal to Chikae, you know, and I respect Dikembe and all…but, I just have to wonder. If we're reduced to fist fights, maybe we need to end this whole war. Just thinking, sis."

"You're tired of it?"

"You know I am. What's gonna happen to our kids, Dee? They grow up like us in this rat hole, all they know is fighting, that's no way to live."

"You think this is an opportunity?"

"Well, could be, but then there's all that dynamite and bombs and such. We have a stockpile, they have a stockpile. It'll keep going."

"What if we could do something about that, I mean, you know, really disarm both sides? What then?"

"Well…it'd give us a chance. But there's no way. We try to blow up their stocks, they'll come at us and we don't even know where they keep theirs."

"Keontae, what if I had a way to do that? Really, I mean. Get rid of both stockpiles. Would you be willing to help?"

"Deiondre! This is…well…treason! If the others heard us, especially Dikembe, we'd be done for!"

"So, keep it quiet! Just tell me, would you help?"

Keontae was quiet for a moment. Then he bent over and whispered in his sister's ear: "You bet I would! You just tell me when and where!"

Deiondre nodded and left without a word. She had her man, now she just needed to make plans with Elu.

Back in the tunnels, Elu and Jackie were reviewing the

maps, in his study. There was a knock at the door. Then Matilda called out: "Elu, Richard is here to see you. I'm sending him in."

Elu looked up to see LH coming into the study.

"What's all this, bishop?" he asked, as he sat down. Richard was very interested in maps and especially the tunnel lay outs. He had studied them before. Although no one had any formal training in things like engineering any more, LH had a knack for it. It just came natural to him.

"Can you read these, LH?" asked Elu. "We're a bit stumped!"

"Well, sure, this is our tunnel system, here. And these are old train tunnels, and some of them are the old rainwater and flood tunnels. I'm always amazed at how elaborate this whole system was. We live in a very small portion of the whole thing. In fact, here, you see, this is one of the levels from our own stair way. It's blocked now, of course, but originally it extended all the way over to the lakeshore. So, why do you have these out?"

"Richard, we have a small problem, but it may become an opportunity, in fact, the opportunity of a lifetime! We need your expertise, though."

"OK, I'm listening, bishop, very interesting so far!"

"This tunnel right here, LH, north of us. See where it's located? Not too far from the river. And, from what I can see, it's very deep, isn't it?"

"Yes, it is. That's the deepest tunnel on that side, in fact."

"And this one, above it. It seems very close to the other one, and it seems like it rides up right along the riverbed. Am I reading this right?"

"You certainly are, bishop. What's this all about, anyway?"

Jackie looked at Elu. Elu nodded. Jackie explained: "This deep tunnel is where the Brigade stores all their explosives. We think we could flood it with a couple of small explosions to break through the tunnel walls. Do you think that's feasible?"

LH's eyes grew wide. He looked at Jackie, then back at Elu, then down again at the map.

"Yes! Yes, it's very possible! The deep tunnel has no other drainage, at least nothing big! It probably has a small drain in the floor but that would be easy to block. The tunnel above it might drain away the water but if the explosions were placed just right, say, here…and here…it would drain right into the deep tunnel. If some barricades were placed in this tunnel, first, that would help. But the real issue is getting in there. We have to figure out where the access points are, and see if they are still open!"

As Richard studied the map, Elu changed to another one.

"Here, LH, look at this one. It's the same thing. This one is very close to the lake, and this one next to it is also very deep. We have good information that the Brotherhood stores their explosive charges in this deep tunnel. We wonder about the same plan."

LH studied the new map.

"Yes, again, bishop! This is a plan that could work. Same thing, we'd have to find the access points, but we can do that, I think. What are you going to use for explosives?"

"Well, we're working on that. I think we may have a lead. I wonder if you could work out the access and all, and maybe soon we could get up to the surface and scope it out. We have a way to do that safely, now."

Richard looked at Elu suspiciously. He knew something strange had been going on. He had no idea what exactly it was, but he trusted the bishop.

"OK, I'm game. I should have this figured out pretty quick, but the real answer is going to be up there, finding which access points are open, and making sure the tunnels are still open and accessible, and all."

"Do what you can, my friend. I think we'll plan a sortie for tomorrow morning. Can you have something by then?"

"I sure can, bishop! Let's plan on it!"

Chapter 35

"Here we are, bishop," called LH. "Over here!"

Elu stumbled across to where Richard LH was standing. It hadn't been an easy trek. They were on the north side of the river, now, and had found an open access hatch. After climbing down a few levels, they were in the tunnel they had identified on the map. The ladders were bad enough for an old man, but there was so much debris and other barriers to walk around and stumble across, that simply walking in a straight line was nearly impossible. Elu didn't even want to stop and think about what all he might be walking through. Fortunately, it was mostly dry, anyway. At least, in the time gap, he didn't have to worry about encountering any little "creatures"!

"Right here. This is the spot. Directly through this wall, about eye level, would be the river! If we blew a hole here, the river would come rushing in!"

"What about the other tunnel?" Elu asked.

"That should be right over here, just about across from it, and about ankle level, I'd say."

Jackie stood there, quietly surveying the whole thing. Richard thumped on the walls, and then she said: "These seem pretty sturdy. You think we can actually blast through here?"

"Well, that'd be up to your explosives specialist, but I can tell you that we're at a dip in the current tunnel. If we have the lower portion open first, the water from the river should pour right into it. There isn't anywhere else for it to go."

"Where else will the water go, though, after the lower tunnel is full? Will it get into other lateral tunnels? The Brigade lives in some of those, although I think they are much closer to the surface than this."

"No, it shouldn't bother them. It will flood some of the

others, but they will be lower ones. Here, I'll mark exactly where to put the charges."

Richard used his torch to smudge the walls in the correct places, and he made some notations on the map he was carrying, then they all climbed back out. Back on the surface, Jackie looked around a bit, then directed the other two to a small, nondescript burnt out building.

"This is it. We can get to the stockpile from here," she told them.

Back down into the tunnels they went, this time with Jackie leading. It was another cumbersome climb down, farther this time, to that deeper tunnel. Soon, however, they were standing in a large room, full of equipment and stacks of things. Elu looked around. Some of the stacks contained large bags of what was labeled as powdered explosives.

"If we flood this room, up to about here," Jackie motioned with her arm to about shoulder height, "that should do it. All the powder will be ruined, and the equipment will be well underwater. It would be too difficult to salvage anything and it wouldn't be useful, anyway, without the powder. Can we get the water up that high?"

"We should be able to," said LH. "There are no lower tunnels or drains that I can see. We should move some of this stuff around, though. There's likely to be at least a small drain or two that we may need to stop up. We can also stack some of this powder down when we need to."

"We should also stack it away from the blast area, so it all doesn't go up!" Elu commented.

"I'll mark the wall again. The explosion should be about… here!" Richard made a smudge about head height on one wall.

"Well, I think that does it. We simply need to figure out the explosives and I'm hoping Deiondre has something for us in that regard," said Elu.

With that, the group trekked back up to the surface, and across the bridge. Elu led them now, as they worked their way into the Brotherhood headquarters, looking for Deiondre. They soon found her, again in the circle of leaders having their morning strategy discussion. This time Elu wasn't as worried about scaring her since they had made plans to meet. He stationed himself across from her again, though, as he had done last time, and then welcomed her into intra-time with the others.

"Bishop, good to see you. Right on time!"

"I have helpers today, behind you. Jackie and LH. Have you met LH?"

Deiondre rose and turned to see them standing there. LH was still a bit surprised at watching this whole intra-time thing, but he was getting used to it.

"I think we met when you were in the tunnel the other day," Richard commented. "Good to see you again. I know Bishop was worried about you when he had his "accident", as he puts it, and had to leave you behind. It was right here, I guess, wasn't it?"

"Yep," answered Elu, wincing a bit. "Not something I prefer to think about just right now, LH!"

LH just grinned at him. "Well, it just proves you're human like the rest of us!"

"I actually didn't need any proof, personally, but thank you anyway!"

Jackie and Deiondre grinned at the two men, and then they got down to business.

"LH has found what we need on the other side, Deiondre," Elu began. "We just need to scope out this side, and then we can make further plans. We still need an explosives expert. Any luck on that front?"

"Actually, yeah, I think so. My brother, Keontae, is pretty

good at that stuff and I had a chat with him yesterday. I think he would be willing to help. It might be good for him to come with us to scout out the tunnels. He should be at his post right now, he's one of our advance scouts."

"OK, then, let's go!" said Elu.

The four of them then trundled back up the stairs and out onto the street. They followed Deiondre, as she worked her way through a couple of side streets, getting closer to the river. Soon, they entered another small building. This one had a second story that was still intact. Up the stairs they went, and found one of the black men from the Brotherhood, sitting by a window, with a good view of the entire river front and over into Brigade territory.

"This is him. How should we approach this?"

"Well," thought Elu out loud, "what all did you tell him?"

"I just said there was a way to do this secretly. He doesn't know anything else."

Elu thought a moment, then had a plan put together. He was getting better at this, although each time was a new adventure!

"LH and Jackie, why don't you wait downstairs for a few minutes. Deiondre, you stand over here, not that close, but where he can see you, and I'll be over in this corner. I'll show up when you "introduce" me."

LH and Jackie left, and Elu and Deiondre took up their positions. Elu then allowed Keontae into the time gap. He saw Deiondre almost immediately.

"What!? Sis, when did you come up here? I didn't even hear you!"

"Concentrating on your job! Good soldier!" Deiondre commented.

"Why are you here?"

"Keontae, remember our discussion yesterday? I said I had a way to do things without the rest knowing about it?"

"Yeah, I remember, but we should probably keep our voices down, you know," Keontae whispered to his sister.

"Well, we actually don't have to do that, Key. I have someone I want you to meet. He's from the tunnels."

"The tunnels? What do you mean?"

"You know the stories. The people who escaped into the tunnels, not part of either faction, waiting for us to win the war or destroy each other."

"Sure, but those are just stories…aren't they?"

Deiondre nodded to Elu, who then slowly walked toward them. Deiondre motioned toward the bishop and told her brother: "See for yourself!"

Keontae turned and had to hold onto the wall to steady himself. He had never seen someone quite like Elu. He wasn't white or black, but somewhere in between. He just stood there gaping at him.

Elu smiled, held out his hands, and said: "It's good to meet you, Keontae. Deiondre has told me about you. My name is Elu."

"How'd you get in here? I must be slipping! I never heard either of you come in!"

"Keontae, you're a good scout, nothing would have escaped your attention, unless something unusual were happening…well, it turns out something unusual did happen!" Elu said.

Keontae looked pretty skeptical, and so Elu invited him to look back out the window.

"What do you see, I mean, the details, you know?" asked Elu.

Keontae stood looking out the window for several moments, then said: "I don't know. It's the same, but not quite…

something's off, but I can't tell what it is..."

"Look at the river. Is it usually that quiet?"

Keontae studied the water, and then looked up and down the river. Then Elu pointed out something else.

"See those gulls over there? What are they doing?"

Keontae stared out the window, looked where Elu was pointing, and shook his head a bit. He closed his eyes, then opened them, and looked again.

"This is very weird," he said, rather slowly. "Those birds aren't moving, and neither is the river. That one gull looks like it's just suspended in midair! What's going on, here?"

"Well, you're right, that gull IS suspended!" Deiondre told him. "That's the bishop's "talent"...he calls it a "gift". He can stop time, Keontae. Don't ask me how, but he can. We can do whatever we need to do, and no one will know anything!"

Keontae spun around and eyed Elu up and down. "What did you call him? He's a bishop? How did you do this? Did you cast some spell?"

Elu chuckled. "Not exactly, Keontae. In fact, I can't give you a full explanation of it, either, but it is a gift I have been given and I have a friend who has helped me develop it. It's quite safe."

As he said these last words, he looked at Deiondre and cocked an eyebrow. She just grinned at him.

"So, brother, are you gonna help us?" she asked him.

"I said I would if you found a way. Looks like you found it. So, what do we do?"

Deiondre and Keontae talked for a while about the layouts and possibilities. She told him about the plan to flood the stockpiles, and stressed that they were going to do the same for the Brigade. He was a bit skeptical about that, at first, but, if it were true, he admitted, he had no problem with the whole thing. All this while, Jackie and Richard LH had been waiting on the lower level. Now, Elu and Deiondre led their new recruit down the stairs, to meet their co-conspirators.

"This is my brother, Keontae. This is Jackie and Richard. They call him LH, for no good reason that I know of," Deiondre said, introducing them.

"Jackie?! You're Jackie Robinson? JCR's wife?" Keontae drew back a bit, instinctively. He looked questioningly at Deiondre.

"Yeah, and she's good, Keontae. She's with us. There's nothing to be afraid of," his sister told him. "Sorry about that," she said to Jackie.

"Hey, not a problem. I'd be more worried if he didn't react like that. It's how we were raised, wasn't it? All of us, except those in the tunnels," Jackie responded.

After the initial shock wore off, Keontae and Deiondre led the group to a nearby building shell, and down, again, into the basement. There were actually several stairways, and they ended up in a "sub-sub-sub-basement". There was then a manhole to uncover and climb down in, and they were in the explosives cache. It wasn't guarded, just like the Brigade's place, simply because it was so isolated.

Richard was quickly able to find their location on the map he was carrying. It seemed to be "as advertised" and he was able to quickly locate a small floor drain, and then found and marked the spot they would need to break through. It was nearly on the ceiling of the room, by one wall. He and Keontae had an animated discussion for a bit but then agreed that they should be able to use a rather small charge and easily breech the wall into the other adjoining tunnel. They simply had to find that tunnel.

It turned out, however, that it really didn't take long. Keontae was a fast learner, as well as a very astute observer. He was able to quickly get them all to the right spot. It was another climb down and then back up, and they had some debris to remove, but finally they stood in the exact spot, as far as they could tell. Richard and Keontae measured and discussed, and finally agreed on the right spot.

"Right here, bishop," said LH. "If we breach here, the water should come pouring in. The opening from below will be right here, and there won't be any obstacles to the water gushing into the explosives hold."

Keontae agreed, and so they set to discussing exactly how to do the deed.

"I can set a charge large enough to blow the wall, but small enough to avoid setting off the other explosives," Keontae related, "but, the fuse will be rather short. We'll have to light it and run!"

Everyone else smiled and Keontae looked around at the other faces.

"What did I say? What's so funny?" he asked.

"Key, remember back at the lookout, when we first showed you how the bishop can stop things?" Deiondre asked. "He can stop time! That should work, I think, right bishop?"

"Yes, Deiondre, that's how it works...or, I should say, doesn't work! What I mean is that nothing mechanical works in the time gap. You can't even strike a match! Whatever you use to light the fuse, we have to come out of the time gap to do it, then, when it's going good, we "freeze" things again, and we have all the "time" we want to leave the area!"

Keontae looked at Elu as if he had three heads, but then he nodded slowly and said: "OK, if you say so...I trust my sister, so I guess I trust you guys, too! So, when do we do this?"

"As soon as we can. We can do it now if you want," Jackie told him.

"Well, not so fast, people," interrupted Elu. "You recall

what I said about needing to rest between episodes, and all that. I am going to have to control this very carefully, and I don't want any slip-ups, like happened last time! I propose we do this first thing tomorrow morning, after I've had a good rest. That should give Keontae plenty of time consider things like how much of a charge he needs, and all that. Is that soon enough, do you all think?"

"It should be OK," said Deiondre. "Our side hasn't come up with anything yet, and, as far as our lookouts can tell, neither has the Brigade. We're still in the "wait and see" mode. We should have a day or two before anything happens."

"And, I think we should have as few of us doing this as we can, just to be safe," said Richard.

The group soon agreed. Tomorrow morning, around the same time, Richard and Elu would meet Keontae at his lookout post, and they would then go around to each place to complete the tasks. Elu then had to go with Keontae and Deiondre to get them properly situated in their previous places, and release them from intra-time. Then he and the other two returned to the tunnels.

Chapter 36

The very next morning, Elu and Richard LH appeared again in Keontae's lookout post. Keontae was there, waiting for them.

"Good morning, my friend," said Elu.

Keontae jumped with a start.

"Bishop, good morning...do you always sneak up on people like that? It's a bit unnerving, even for a seasoned lookout like me!" Keontae blurted out.

"Sorry, I'm just not quite used to this, even yet! But, here we are, ready to go to work! I hope you are, too."

"I am, and I've been studying the plans. I think it should work fine. Oh, good morning, LH! I didn't see you there at first!"

LH just smiled. "Yeah, the bishop seems to take center stage, especially when he scares people like that!"

The three of them decided to start in the Brotherhood storeroom. They could have started across the river, but Keontae knew the south side much better and thought the first run should be where he knew the layout. That made sense to the others, and so off they went to the storeroom. They were in for a bit of a surprise, however.

When they got to the storeroom, there was already a bit of light coming from inside. They carefully looked in, and saw several of the children. One of them had a torch, and he was standing rather close to the bags of TNT!

"Now what do we do?!" asked LH.

Elu took a deep breath, and thought for a moment.

"Keontae," he said after a pause, "do you know these kids?"

Keontae had been peering at them, and then nodded.

"These are the ones that are usually causing problems. They like to sneak into places they're not allowed. That one is Dikembe's son."

"What do you suggest we do?"

"If you two hide, I can go in and shoo them away. They know they aren't supposed to be there, and I'll threaten to tell their parents if they talk at all."

That seemed to be a good idea, so Elu and LH positioned themselves in an adjacent small room, which had a door they left a bit ajar. Elu let them all out of intra-time and Keontae could then hear the kids giggling as they played. He entered the room with his own torch. The men had special torches for when they entered the storeroom. These torches had glass coverings, to reduce the risk of an explosion. The kids, of course, simply had an old regular torch.

"What are you kids doing in here!" Keontae shouted. "Get that torch out of here! Don't you know you'll blow the whole place sky high?!"

The kids froze in fright, and the one with the torch almost dropped it. Keontae ran over to him and grabbed the torch, taking it away from the bags of explosive.

"Get outta here before I drag you all back to your parents! You know what they'll do if they knew you were in here! Come back again, and it's all over for you guys!"

Of course, the kids ran like crazy out of the storeroom. Keontae took the offending torch into the hallway and set it up in one of the holders they had there. Then he noticed the torch suddenly stopped wavering, and he realized Elu must have done the "time thing" again. Just then, Elu and LH stepped out of their hiding place.

"Good job, Keontae!" Elu commented. "Are they far enough away by now, do you think?"

"They was goin' like bats out of he...oops, sorry, bishop,

like nuts…I'm sure they're well away from here by now," Keontae said.

"OK, then, lads, let's see what we can do, here," said Elu as he led them into the storeroom.

Keontae looked around a bit, and picked out what he needed.

"That's a lot of explosive!" said LH.

"Well, it has to do for at least four blows! I don't know what all I'll find in the north, so I'd rather bring my own, you know!"

That made sense to the other two, so they helped Keontae with his load. They carried it all into the outer hallway. Then Keontae separated out the charge he needed for this level and took it back into the storeroom. He set the charge where they had marked it the day before, and set the fuse.

"Now, friends, we have some work to do. These bags of dynamite are simply too close to this wall. We have to move them back at least a bit, to prevent them all going off with this charge," he told the others.

That took them a while, but soon they had all the bags stacked down, to make sure the water would cover them all, and away from the wall, so they wouldn't ignite when the smaller charge went off.

"So, Keontae, how exactly do you light this thing?" asked Elu.

"Well, we do have matches, but a very tiny supply. I'd rather not use them, because we use them for lighting torches, too. But, I do have a small flint igniter, and the sparks it makes are normally good enough, if you hold it just right. You have to know how to use it, you know."

With that, Keontae pulled a long metal gadget out of his shirt pocket. It had two metal arms, with a cup at the end. He couldn't get it to work, for some reason.

"Oops, sorry," said Elu. "I forgot. We have to be out of the time gap for anything mechanical to work. Let's do that and see if it'll work."

Elu dropped them out of intra-time, and Keontae tried again. This time, when he squeezed the arms together quickly, holding them just right, sparks flew out of the cup. He grinned at Elu, then bent over the fuse he had just set. Soon it was burning just right. Elu re-entered intra-time, and the flame froze in place.

"Now, we need to get out of here, gentlemen!" Elu announced. They ran quickly out of the storeroom, and gathered up their other explosives. They headed for the upper levels, and went all the way back to Keontae's post. Since they weren't sure what this would be like, they wanted to be in a safe and secure location.

Then, in the lookout station, Elu looked at the other two men and asked if they were ready for this. They nodded and the three of them slipped out of intra-time. They waited for several seconds, then felt a sudden shuddering and heard a muffled "boom".

"I think it's time to examine our handiwork, men!" exclaimed Elu.

Since the whole point of this exercise was to open a channel from the tunnel near the water, they decided to check on the results from that upper tunnel. Elu had dropped them back into the time gap as soon as the shuddering had stopped. Now, in a very short time, they were back at the site of the explosion, but looking down at it from above. Sure enough, they had a nice hole opened up between the two sites. The locations LH and Keontae had marked were just right. A hole several feet wide now existed in the lower part of the upper tunnel wall, and it dropped directly into the storeroom.

"This should be perfect!" Shouted Elu. "Are you ready for the next one?"

Keontae soon had the new charge set. He had brought a double charge for this site. There weren't any bags of TNT to worry about and he wanted to be really sure it would work. The whole process was repeated, with the lighting of the fuse and the men scurrying out of the tunnel. As they were hurrying along, it occurred to Elu that they really didn't need to hurry, since they were in intra-time, but it just seemed like the right thing to do, "just in case".

Again, up in the watchtower, they returned to normal space-time, and waited. Soon, again, there was a "boom" and a shudder, although this time much more violent. That seemed to be right, since it was a larger charge, and closer to the surface, although it startled them just a bit.

"Well, let's go see!" said Elu.

"Wait, just a moment, bishop. We need to give the water time to flow into the tunnel, too, you know."

"Oh, that makes sense!" So, Elu waited a bit before he had them back into the time gap.

This time, they went all the way back down to the store-room to check things out. They were almost down the stairs to that level when they encountered water.

"This is about where I thought it should be, bishop!" said LH.

Elu smiled and kept going into the water.

"Bishop! Wait, what are you doing? You can't go down there!" said LH.

"Oh, but I can!" grinned Elu. "I've done this before! I don't need to breathe when I'm in the time gap, you know!"

LH considered this for a moment, then, with a raised eyebrow, he commented: "OK, but what are you gonna use for light?

Will the torch work down there?"

Elu stopped. He hadn't considered that.

"I don't know! I guess we can see!" He took the torch, the special one with the glass covering, from Keontae, and very slowly descended into the water. He felt the top of the door, just beneath the surface, and very carefully lowered himself and the torch down and into the storeroom. He was back rather quickly.

"Hey, come on, you two! This works fine!" he yelled back to his comrades. Soon, they were all three in the storeroom. Elu was able to hold the torch high enough that it was out of the water. The water was up to the top of the doorway, and covered everything in the place. They could see pretty well, with the torch above the water. It didn't give quite as good illumination when it was submerged, but it did work. They walked all the way around the room and then back up the stairway.

"Wow, bishop," exclaimed Keontae, "that was awesome!"

"Fun, wasn't it? And, your explosives worked just fine! This "arms depot" is officially out of business! They'll never be able to use this stuff against anybody. Time to get over to the north side!"

The three hurried back up to the surface, noticing that their clothes were wet, but not as much as they would have expected! It was certainly a strange experience, they all thought.

Chapter 37

Elu stressed to his friends that they had better get up to the north and get the job done there, also, as soon as they could. It was very likely the Brigade had heard the explosions and had some idea of what was going on. They would either decide to attack the Brotherhood, or they would set a guard on their own cache of explosives, or both. Elu wanted to get the thing taken care of before they could react. Of course, they were in the time gap, and didn't really need to "hurry", but Elu didn't want to take any chances. If this took too long, he was worried he could drop out of intra-time before they were ready and maybe not be able to re-enter it right away.

It wasn't long before they were at the Brigade's explosives site, and their fears were realized. There were several men there, a couple in the storeroom itself, and one stationed outside in the hallway, guarding the entry.

"Now, what, bishop?" asked Keontae.

Elu studied the situation for a moment. He wasn't exactly sure the best way to handle it.

"Well," he started, "there's only three of them. We could simply carry them away. We could get out of the time gap and scare them away. What do you guys think?"

"Can't we just leave them there?" asked Keontae. "I don't think they are quite close enough to be harmed by the explosion, and they should be able to run quick enough once the water starts coming in."

"I'm not so sure," offered LH. "They may be knocked over by either one, but the other problem is, what if they see the fuse going and realize what's happening? They might have enough time to stop the explosion."

Keontae admitted that might be true. Finally, they decided to simply try to carry them away. They only needed to be down the hallway a bit to be safe. They started with the fellow in the hallway, to see how far they could move him. With all three of them, it didn't take too much, and soon he was ensconced in a side room, a ways down from the storeroom. They went back and soon had the others moved, too. Then they went through the same procedure again with moving the TNT and setting and lighting the charge.

Back on the surface, they allowed the explosion to occur, and then hustled down into the upper tunnel by the water. They could see into the storeroom and it seemed like the hole in the wall had been opened like it had been on the south side.

"Wait a minute," said LH. He leaned over and stuck the torch into the room deeper. Then he jumped back with a bit of a squeal!

"Whoa!" he cried.

"What?" asked Elu.

"Sorry, but I saw a face! It was one of those men. He was staring right at me!"

The three of them then carefully peered into the hole and held out the torch into the darkness. There they were! All three of the men they had moved were back and staring at the hole in the wall!

"How did they get here so quickly?" asked Keontae.

"Well," said Elu, "they must have started moving as soon as we lit the fuse. They would have gotten halfway back to the storeroom when the explosion went off, and I must have been slower than I thought getting back into intra-time! Anyway, we're going to have to move them again, to be safe! Probably farther away this time, so they can't get back here before the water comes pouring in!"

LH and Keontae dropped down into the storeroom, and Elu handed them the torch. He was about to swing down himself when LH stopped him.

"Bishop, no, Keontae and I can do this. No sense hurting yourself! We can take care of them."

Elu reluctantly agreed, and so he sat there in the darkness for a while. Soon, the torch light returned, and he was able to help the other two back up through the hole without too much trouble. They went through the same process and soon were on their way back down to the storeroom to see how it went.

At the bottom of the stairs, the water was high, again, as it had been on the Brotherhood side. This time, however, there were three men coming up the stair way to greet them! They were "frozen" on the stairs, and they were a bit wet, but they were safe and unharmed. Apparently their plan had worked on the Brigade side just as it had down south. Just to be sure, Keontae took the torch and went by himself to check. He was soon back with a good report. All the explosives were in the water and nothing was salvageable.

Soon, Keontae was back at his post, as if nothing had happened. Elu and LH retreated to the tunnels, and Elu allowed them all out of the time gap. Now it was just a matter of waiting to see how the factions on the surface would respond to the loss of their explosive caches.

Chapter 38

"Keontae, can you explain what you were doing in the storeroom right before the explosion?" Dikembe glared at the lookout as he asked the question. Everyone else in the leadership circle was caught off guard and looked back and forth between Keontae and his accuser with their eyes wide with surprise.

Keontae was silent for a moment, which led Chikae to ask his lieutenant a question.

"Dikembe, what are you talking about?"

"I have it on good authority that Keontae was seen in the munitions room before that explosion. He had no authority to be there."

Everyone looked back at Keontae. He simply shrugged and said: "I don't know what your "good authority" is, Dikembe, but you can check the logs and ask the other watchmen. I was at my post that morning, the entire time. I even felt the explosion myself, and ran out to ask Kofi what it was."

Actually, Keontae had done that. As soon as he got back to his post, after all the commotion, he came running out as if he were as surprised as anyone else, and asked his fellow watchmen what was happening. There was a bit of a time lag there, but not enough for them to notice. Elu had done a good job of managing the time gap.

Kofi nodded. "That is what happened, Dikembe. Keontae was as startled as the rest of us."

Dikembe snarled a bit and dropped his questioning.

"Well, Dikembe, if we're gonna get to the bottom of this, you need to find out from your "sources" who they really saw," suggested Chikae. "In the meantime, there's not a lot of point in going over that. We need to decide what to do with this situation. What do we know about the Brigade?"

Kofi spoke up again. Besides being a watchman, he was also one of the scouts. He had snuck across the river, and done a bit of recon after the second series of explosions.

"As far as I can tell, there was no one from the Brigade on our side of the river, and none of us were on their side. The explosions and flooding we experienced happened on the north side, also. They are also now without any ammunition or explosives. It appears we are both in the same boat, and no one knows why or who was responsible."

The group simply sat there, staring at the floor or one another. No one had an explanation or any suggestions as to what they should do next. Dikembe made a few comments about "taking it out" on the Brigade, but no one took him seriously, and even he was half-hearted about it.

In the meantime, to the north, a similar discussion was taking place deep within in the Brigade's territory.

"What do you mean, we're defenseless?!" shouted JCR. "We must have something stored somewhere! We just need to find it!"

"I don't think so, JC," said Churchy. "It's all gone. You remember, we had decided a long time ago, to centralize the whole thing. We've been wiped out. The good news is, as far as we can tell, the Brotherhood has the same problem. Somebody did it to them, too!"

"That makes no sense!" claimed JCR. "There isn't anyone else, except that old friar, and he's no threat! Who would've done this!"

No one answered. No one had any ideas. JCR, of course, knew there were others. His encounter with Elu on the bridge proved that. But, he hadn't told anyone else about it. It would have meant admitting he was bested by an old man and a woman, and that was the last thing he was prepared to do.

Suddenly, JCR shouted: "I know! It's Jackie! She's getting back at us! It must be her, who else would it be?"

"JC, I don't think she could have pulled off something like this, even with the friar's help. She doesn't know much about that kind of thing. It would have taken some pretty good engineering smarts to do this! Besides, how do you account for the stories of our men who were doing the inventory at the same time? They didn't see anyone, and yet they were repeatedly moved out of the storeroom, as if someone didn't want them hurt in the explosion!"

Then someone else piped up: "JC, I thought you told us the Brotherhood had killed your family! Isn't that what happened?"

Realizing he had been caught in a lie, JCR paused a moment, then blurted out: "I'm sure they did, but I bet Jackie told them all about how to pull this off before she died...they probably tortured it out of her!"

Everyone looked at each other as they began to realize that a lot of this was in JCR's imagination. The meeting slumped into an uncomfortable silence, just like the gathering south of them. In the tunnels, however, it was a different story. There, Elu and LH, and Jackie were rejoicing.

"It went very well, Jackie. Much better than we expected, in fact. All those munitions are under water and will never be used again!"

"I hope Deiondre and Keontae are going to be OK. I hope no one suspects them," she said.

Elu paused, then he looked Jackie in the eye and said: "Do you realize what you just said, Jackie? You're worried about two new friends, who used to be mortal enemies! There is hope for our world!"

Jackie smiled, even though she was trying not to. "Yes," she said, "you're right, I guess. I think the three of us, especially Deiondre and I, have a lot in common. I never would have expected that, and I never would have found it out if it weren't for you and Leo."

Elu looked over at Leo, who was back, again, enjoying Matilda's cooking. He just grinned back at his bishop.

"So, now what do we do," asked Jackie.

Elu sat back in his chair and twiddled his thumbs a bit, as he thought.

"Well, we're just doing this one step at a time, you know. Frankly, I don't know, but it depends a bit on the reactions we get. I would suggest, though, that we can do a bit of spying. Leo, perhaps you can get a bit of a sense from the kids and the moms you run into. I'll have to visit Deiondre and Keontae, probably tomorrow, to give them a bit of time to digest things. Then we can see what all we need to do."

Chapter 39

Elu showed up again, as usual, at the Brotherhood council, standing across from Deiondre. She saw him and smiled, as he brought her into intra-time. She ran over to him and embraced him!

"You did it, bishop! All the stores are destroyed! I hope it is the same with the Brigade," she exclaimed.

"It is, Deiondre. All the weapons are destroyed. Of course, they can make new cruder ones, knives, and all, but the worst of them are gone and it will take time to make others. How's it going here?"

"As I suspected. Chikae is bewildered. Dikembe is incensed! He wants to attack the Brigade. He's certain they had something to do with all this. The rest of them are more cautious. Keontae was blamed at first, but Dikembe had no evidence and my brother was able to deflect it. What should we do now?"

"What I would like to see, Deiondre, is that they all come to the understanding that this whole thing raises possibilities for them. Possibilities for ending the violence and hate. What are the chances of that?"

"Some of them are already there. I know many of the women are. I am the only woman on the council, but I can press the issue," she responded.

"Do what you can to do that, Deiondre. I suspect it would be best for me to not be seen, at least for now. I think this needs to come as sort of a "grass-roots" movement, and I can help facilitate a meeting between the factions when the time is right for it. I don't think it should wait long, but it has to "ripen", as it were. Would that work, you think?"

"Yes, bishop. Give me a day or two. If you could plan to

meet me here each morning like this, I can give you an update and we can work toward that. Is that OK with you?"

"I think it's a wonderful plan, Deiondre! If you need something before I return, perhaps you or Keontae could contact me. Either come down the stairway or seek out Brother Leo. But, be careful!"

"We will, bishop. Thank you for all you've done, so far. I'll talk to you tomorrow."

With that, Deiondre went back to her place, smiled up at Elu, and then bowed her head to get back into position in the council. Elu allowed her to slip out of the time gap, and headed back home.

At home, he didn't have to wait long for Leo to show up. Jackie was there, also, waiting anxiously to hear from him.

"My brother, what did you find out?" Elu asked as soon as Leo was in the door.

"Bishop, it's very interesting. I have only second-hand information, of course, from some of the older children and a couple of the women. One of the women was very helpful. She is Maureen, the wife of the man they call "Churchy"."

"Oh, I know Maureen, of course. She's very good. She knows more than any other of the women what goes on in the leaders' group. Churchy tells her everything. She's a very strong woman and has been agitating for change for quite a while, actually," said Jackie.

"Good to know," commented Elu. "What did she tell you, Leo?"

"Maureen says the leaders are divided. JCR is adamant that they should attack the Brigade, even though they have no weapons. No one's taking him seriously, and he's losing the confidence of the others. Most of them are simply confused and bewildered. Churchy apparently believes some "outside force" is at work, but he has no way to know what or who. Oh, and JCR blames you, Jackie. The rest of them think that's crazy, but JCR won't let it go!"

"This is similar to the report I got from Deiondre about the Brotherhood," said Elu. "Do you think Maureen is strong enough that we could support her to bring the rest of them to understand the possibilities here? You know, Leo, as you said before, that this is an opportunity, not a threat?"

"I know she is," said Jackie. "She and I had a good relationship. I'm sure I could speak to her."

Elu thought about it for a moment. Then he had a plan.

"Leo, do you think you could get Maureen to come to the friary and meet with you and Jackie? I could be there, if you think it necessary, to provide "time cover" or something."

"I don't think that would be necessary, bishop. I agree Maureen is a strong woman and she and Jackie could probably work things out, if we simply get them together. Let me see what I can do. I told her I would be back possibly later today, and we could even meet this evening at the friary. I hate to let it go too far out, you know."

"When do you want me there, Leo?" asked Jackie.

"Let's see, if you use the sundial, let's plan for around 4 pm. That way we can be done and you can get back here before dark."

"Are you sure you don't need me to help?" asked Elu. He was feeling a bit "useless" but more importantly, he simply wanted to be sure everyone was safe!

"No, bishop, I know the area better than you do, and I can get back and forth safely. No worries."

Leo left in a hurry, then, to get back to Maureen and arrange the meeting. Jackie had to go check on her kids. Elu was left to simply worry! He decided to go pray!

Chapter 40

"Hi, Jackie, how are you?" asked Maureen, as Jackie entered the friary.

Leo was waiting there, also, and the two of them were sitting on the small pews, facing one another. Maureen was situated facing the door. Jackie smiled and sat down on another pew, facing both of them. It became a triangle.

"I'm doing well, Maureen. And you? How are the kids?"

"Doing OK, Jackie. Missing Tommy and Leah. I heard you were hurt pretty bad. Are you all better, now?"

"I am. My new friends have taken good care of me and the kids are in school, believe it or not!"

This news seemed to shock Maureen, but she recovered quickly.

"We had been told you died and the kids were slaves of the Brotherhood! But, that came from JC and, frankly, nobody believes him anymore."

"That's not much of a surprise. He says what he wants people to believe. It was just a matter of time before everybody got wise to him."

"Have you given up on him, Jackie?"

Jackie had to pause. She hadn't actually faced that question, at least not directly and not yet. She had to think.

"I don't know, Maureen…I mean, yeah, he and I, you know, we're not together anymore and we never will be. I don't see how that could ever happen."

"It's sad, but I understand. If you wanted to get back with him, I'd argue against it, you know."

Jackie smiled again. Maureen was tough, but a good friend.

She always told the truth, as she saw it, and never beat around the bush much.

"How are you and Churchy?"

"We're good, but Churchy is struggling with this whole thing. Everybody is starting to look up to him more than JC, but he's still loyal to him. "He's our leader, Maureen, we have to respect him…" he keeps saying. I think he's saying it more to himself than to me."

"What are they planning to do? I hear the Brigade and the Brotherhood are completely disarmed, now. Have they decided anything?"

"No. JC wants to mount an attack. I think he just wants to fight somebody, and he doesn't care who it is. He's just mad as hell…oops, sorry, Brother Leo…it just came out!"

"No problem, Maureen," chuckled Leo. "Last I checked, hell was still a real place…and it's NOT here, by the way!"

Both women had to smile at that.

"You know, Leo, it's interesting you say that," commented Maureen. "Because, these last few years, it's seemed like hell! What can we do to change that? Do we have a new chance now? Have we been handed some sort of "get out of jail" card or something?"

"Maybe we have, Maureen," answered Jackie. "What if we played it that way? What would the rest of the Brigade say? What would the rest of the women say? Would they be with us?"

"Most of them would be. I know I can count on several of them, and a lot of the others could be persuaded. There are a few hot heads, of course, but the women would mostly be behind it. I think most of the men would be, too! We have to deal with some hard liners, but Churchy can handle them. What did you have in mind?"

"When's the next women's gathering? Are you still having

those?"

"Oh, yeah. I took them over when you left. We meet again tomorrow morning, in fact. Same place, and all."

"I want to be there, Maureen. Would that be OK? You and I together, I think we can convince them, and then get the men behind us."

Maureen shook her head, not to disagree, but just to clear her mind. This was a big gamble.

"You sure about that? It's not the safest thing for you to do! I can do it, but, I agree, it would be more forceful with both of us there."

"If I'm not willing to take a risk, why should we ask the rest of them to? Besides, it's for the kids, right?"

"It is. Let's do it! I hope you have a plan, though, to take to the men. They won't react well to just a pie in the sky idea, you know."

"Oh, I have a plan, alright! Just wait, you'll like it!" said Jackie.

Maureen left, then, to wait for the next morning. Jackie left for the tunnels, and Leo stayed in his friary. He had the same idea as Elu. He spent the whole night praying for all of them.

Chapter 41

That evening, Jackie debriefed Elu on her visit with Maureen.

"We have a clear path, I think, bishop. Maureen is with us and she has a good read on the other women. I have some ideas, but I need to discuss it with Deiondre. What do you think about her and I getting together soon?"

"She seemed to have a good handle on things, too, but needed a day or two. I agreed to meet her each morning. I can relay the request to her tomorrow. What exactly do you want me to suggest to her?"

"I'm still working it out in my own head, but I think she and I can hammer out something when we meet."

"I'll see what I can do," promised Elu.

The very next morning, Elu was back at the Brotherhood headquarters, and Deiondre was in her customary spot. Elu allowed her into the time gap, and they chatted.

"So, how are things going, Deiondre?" Elu asked.

"I think we are about there, bishop. Many of the women have told me, in secret, of course, that they agree and want to see the whole feud over with. How's it going with Jackie?"

"Very much the same, frankly! She wants to meet with you. She has some plans, but hasn't formulated them enough to tell me about them. What do you think about a meeting?"

"It's time, bishop. We have all we need here. I agree, she and I need to talk. When can we do that?"

"Well, we could do it right now, if you want! We can just walk back to the tunnels, and get together with her. If we do it all in intra-time, we don't have to worry about what's going on here. You won't be missed, at all."

"OK, then, let's go!" Deiondre responded.

Elu was excited about all the enthusiasm. He felt good about how these two strong women were developing. He and Deiondre hurried out to the street and over to the stairway. They descended the stairs quickly, and soon found Jackie waiting for them with Matilda. Jackie had suspected that Deiondre might return with Elu and so she had come over to visit. She had just gotten back from her early morning meeting with Maureen and the rest of the Brigade women. It had gone well, and she had ideas to discuss with Deiondre.

As Elu entered, he allowed Jackie and Matilda both into intra-time. He was a bit surprised at how quickly they responded. Apparently everyone was getting used to Elu doing this.

"Aha, I thought you two would be back here, soon!" Exclaimed Jackie.

"Would the two of you like some breakfast before you start all your talking?" asked Matilda.

"Thank you, but, no, I ate already back home," replied Deiondre. "Besides, I think Jackie and I are a bit anxious to talk, right, Jackie?"

"Well, I sure am," Jackie responded. "Where can we sit? Bishop, could we use your study?"

"Well, there's really not a lot of room in there..." Elu started. He was cut off by Jackie.

"We only need space for two! This should be just between Deiondre and I, if that's OK with you, bishop!"

"Oh, well...sure, if that's the best way..." Elu was a bit apprehensive, but Deiondre seemed to agree, and so he let them use his study. He kept them both in the time gap, so Deiondre wouldn't be missed back at her place, and he kept Matilda in, just to give himself some company! That turned out to be a good idea, because the two women conferred together for what seemed like a very long "time". Finally, they emerged.

"We have a plan!" gushed Jackie. "Bishop, could you be at Keontae's lookout post tomorrow morning, about mid-morning or so? And, bring Brother Leo."

"I can. What else do you need me to do."

"That's it, we've got the rest...oh, and no "time travel" or "gap" or whatever, this time, OK?"

"Um, sure. What exactly do you have in mind?"

The two smiled and looked at each other a moment, then Deiondre replied: "I guess you'll just have to be there to see!"

Elu was quite surprised, but then he remembered what he had thought earlier about the two strong women. He realized he needed to simply trust them. He and Deiondre left, then, to get her back to the Brotherhood without some kind of time discrepancy showing up.

Chapter 42

As Elu promised, he and Brother Leo showed up at Keontae's post the next morning. Elu did use intra-time just to get there, and then just slipped out of it when they were with Keontae. Both he and Leo were a bit nervous being there without the time gap protection. Leo, however, was more used to it, and Elu kept reminding himself that he needed to trust in his new friends.

"So, what's going on this morning, bishop?" asked Keontae. "Deiondre said you'd be here, but she didn't tell me anything about what or why."

"Frankly, Keontae, I have no idea, really! They didn't tell me."

"They? Who's "they"?"

"Your sister and Jackie. They met at my place yesterday to plan all of this."

Keontae was a bit surprised but he, also, was used to his sister doing unexpected things, and they usually worked out, so he was willing to just wait and see.

They didn't need to wait long. Very soon, another couple of lookouts came running in. They were momentarily stunned when they saw Elu and Leo, but then caught themselves, when they saw Keontae wasn't uptight about it.

"Keontae, look out the other side!" One of them said.

The lookout room had two sides. One side, where Keontae normally was stationed, looked north across the river. The other side, accessed through a door, had a window that looked east, toward the lake. The whole group ran into that room and peered out the window.

"Who is that?" asked Elu. His eyesight was not as good as

the younger men's.

"Oh, my God!" exclaimed Keontae. "I hope she knows what she's doing!"

He turned to Elu and explained: "It's Deiondre, with Jackie Robinson. They're holding hands, and standing in the middle of the bridge!"

Elu squinted and thought he could identify them. He almost fainted. Then, he turned and ran toward the door. He ran smack into Leo. The friar was blocking the door.

"Leo, move! I have to get to them! What they're doing is dangerous! I've got to stop this, before something bad happens."

Elu had realized that it was simply too far away to bring the two women into intra-time, at least reliably. He was also so agitated that he simply didn't think to just get into the time gap himself and then go down there.

Leo didn't budge.

"Bishop, no, we need to let this play out!"

"Leo, what did they tell you?"

"Nothing more than they told you, excellency. But, I just know we can't interfere, not now. We have to trust them!"

Elu paused a moment. That was exactly what he had been telling himself for the last couple of days. He realized Leo was right, and so reluctantly turned back to the window.

On the north side, the Brigade lookout had also sounded the alarm, and soon the entire leadership group was standing there, looking down at the two women on the bridge. They weren't sure what to do or what it meant.

"This is our chance," shouted JCR. "We need to go down there and capture those two! Then we'll have some real leverage on those guys!"

No one budged. Most of them glanced at Churchy, who was

just standing there watching the spectacle outside. After a few moments, he turned to JCR.

"I think we should wait and see what happens. I'm sure they have more than just this planned."

"I said attack!" shouted JCR. "Are you gonna ignore a direct order?"

"You want us to attack a couple of women? I say we wait." Churchy retorted.

JCR just glared at him, when suddenly the lookout cried: "Look, there's more!"

As the men watched, abruptly a couple of other women from their own side came onto the bridge. They walked up and one of them took Jackie's free hand, and then the hand of her companion. There were now four women standing in the middle of the bridge, holding hands. They looked as if they were saying something, or maybe singing, but the men couldn't hear anything from that distance.

On the south side, a similar scene was playing out. This time, it was the second in command, Dikembe, who wanted to intervene and grab hostages. Chikae stared him down, but Dikembe seemed very angry about the whole thing. He tried to stir up the rest, and there were a few who seemed sympathetic to his cries, until something else happened. Suddenly, every man in the Brotherhood (except those with Keontae at the lookout post) stood rooted to the floor, watching in amazement.

As all of them watched, there was a sudden flow of figures. Dozens of women, from both ends of the bridge, came rushing into the middle of the platform. They held hands, some, but most of them just bustled around the leaders. They were jumping up and down, and singing. Now they could hear it, but couldn't quite make out much.

"They're charging each other," yelled Dikembe! "We need to go down and help them!"

"No," shouted Chikae, firmly. "This is not at attack. Look at them, Dikembe. Take a good look, brother! They're singing together. It's not an attack, it's a rally! The women, from both sides, are rallying against US! I don't think they need us to help. I think they want us to join them!"

Back at the south lookout post, Keontae and his comrades, along with Elu and Leo, were also standing there, speechless, watching all of this unfold.

"Come on, guys," exclaimed Keontae. "We need to get down there! We need to join them, we need to support the women!"

He and his lookout colleagues ran down the stairs. Leo and Elu followed after, at a slightly slower pace, of course.

Soon, in fact, all the men from the Brotherhood were standing at the foot of the bridge, on the south side, and all the Brigade men were gathered on their end. Elu and Leo hurried along and brought up the rear on the south. It was then that Elu recognized what the women were singing. He had heard this song years ago, but it was something that wasn't used much anymore. It had an immediate effect on him. He and Leo began to sing along: "We shall overcome..."

Soon, even some of the men began to sing along, at least on the south side. Elu couldn't tell but it seemed like the men from the north were joining in. It wasn't long before the singing stopped. Jackie and Deiondre stepped out of the crowd of women, and moved to the railing, in the center of the bridge, where everyone could see them. They looked over the assembled crowd, both ends, and in the middle. Then Jackie spoke up, loud enough for everyone to hear.

"We have been living under a cloud. A cloud of fear, a cloud of danger, a cloud that prevents us from becoming what we could be. This cloud has ruined lives and families and it threatens to ruin us and our children. We can't allow that to happen. We AREN'T going to let it happen! It's up to all of us. Are we willing to step into the sunshine, or do we want to end our lives huddled in hiding places, fearing the next attack? It's up to us."

Then Deiondre added: "I, for one, am tired of living like this! My children deserve better! We all deserve better! Who's with us?"

All the women began to shout, with their hands raised into the air. Some of the men did, as well. After that died down, Deiondre looked across at the Brotherhood men.

"Brothers, are you committed to this? Are you willing to end this violence, and join your sisters?"

There was a nearly unanimous shout of agreement from the Brotherhood, pointedly excluding Dikembe, who stood there with his arms folded, and a grim look on his face.

Jackie then turned to her side. "And what about you, my own people? Are you ready, also?"

Again, there was a loud shout of agreement.

Jackie then continued: "I challenge you, then, you leaders. Come up here right now, and pledge yourselves to one another, to work for peace and form a united people!"

There was a pause, then Chikae, with one or two of his closest lieutenants, came walking up. Dikembe refused to go. On the other side, there was a brief scuffle, but then Churchy came up with a couple of men. Elu could see JCR standing there, being restrained by several other men. He apparently had tried to keep Churchy from responding to the women's call. Chikae and Churchy met in the center of the bridge. They looked suspiciously at one another, then, abruptly, they embraced. Everyone cheered. Elu could no longer hold back his tears!

Chapter 43

"That was pretty dramatic, you two!" said Elu, when he had the chance to meet up with Jackie and Deiondre. "I wish you had told me what you were planning!"

"Sure, then you would have stopped us!" replied Jackie.

Elu grinned and nodded. She was right. He had a lot to learn about trust, and letting go control of things, he mused.

"What now?" he asked.

"Well," Deiondre said, "we have agreed to have a meeting of the leadership teams of both sides, and talk about how to go about this, but I think we'll become all one group, now. We have a few rebels, as you probably noticed. But, that's life. We'll get through it. It's just too bad it took so long, and required so much, but now it's done. We're all better off because of it, and we have you to thank, bishop."

"Well, I suspect it would have happened anyway, without me. After all, as I would say, it seems to have been a work of the Spirit. However, I guess it happened sooner than it would have, and that's a good thing."

Just then, Maureen walked up, along with Churchy.

"Bishop," said Jackie, "this is Maureen, and her husband Churchy. I think Churchy is now the head of the Brigade since JCR went sort of ballistic at the bridge!"

"It's good to finally meet you, bishop," said Maureen. Churchy also greeted Elu and shook his hand.

"I don't know if I'm the leader of anything, frankly." Churchy declared. "It all depends, really, on how things work out. I think we need to start fresh and regroup all our leadership ideas. What do you think, Chikae?"

Churchy was calling across the room, and Chikae, hearing

his name, came over and met Elu, also. Everyone already knew Leo, who tried to keep to the periphery. The friar was never comfortable in the center of things, anyway. He figured that was the bishop's role.

"I agree, Churchy. You know, bishop, we've been fighting all our lives, and making up stories about each other, to stoke the hate. But, despite it all, we really know a lot more about our so-called adversaries than you might think. Churchy and I have met several times, on the "battlefield", you might say. We know one another's kids and wives, and everything. It's like a family feud, and I, for one, am glad it's over!"

Everyone agreed with that, but then Churchy made a comment.

"Not everyone agrees with us, I know, but I do believe we can do this. The nay-sayers, and you know who they are, are already saying it can't be done. But you know what? We can do this. If it falls apart, it's our own fault. This thing can work if we allow it. It won't be perfect and we'll have rough spots and even vigorous disagreements, but if we work at it, if we really believe it's important, if we truly respect each other, it can work. We simply need to not give up!"

"You're more of a leader than you realize, my friend," commented Chikae, "and I completely agree with you! Besides, if we give up, guess what? The women won't let us get away with it! Am I right?"

Everyone laughed but they all knew Chikae was right.

"What role do want to play in all this, bishop?"

"Oh, my, I think I've done my part. As far as I'm concerned, it's up to you guys. I do think the folks in the tunnels should be part of whatever you create up here. We don't want any more divisions! We can't afford that. Division breeds misunderstanding and misunderstanding breeds hatred, and then we're back where we just came from. But, for me, I'm happy to just be the spiritual guide. I have a dream about rebuilding the old cathedral here on the surface, and teaching and sanctifying, and all that a bishop is expected to do."

"Well, bishop, we're having a leadership meeting tomorrow afternoon. We plan to start right here on the bridge. Can you have someone from your place join us? I think that would be the place to start."

"I have several people in mind, Chikae. I'll make sure they're here. You can bet on it!"

As the people on the bridge continued to mill about, beginning, or re-starting relationships, Elu and Leo quietly slipped away, certain that their efforts had been successful, but that now it was to be the work of the people and the Spirit.

Chapter 44

The next morning, Elu was in his study, relaxing, and musing about recent events. It was a remarkable turn of fortunes and he was rather pleased with the whole thing. Suddenly, he was startled back to reality. Adeevan appeared abruptly, simply standing there, looking down at him.

"Adeevan! My friend! It's been too long, it's good to see you!" he exclaimed.

Adeevan smiled at the bishop.

"Yes, it has been a while. I left you alone. You were busy. And, quite successful, I might add. You have done well, my friend."

Elu felt rather full of himself, with a tinge of guilt for the pride involved, but just smiled at his mentor. Adeevan continued.

"This age is a tremendous challenge, elder, and you have been able to provide your people with a ray of hope. Not easy to do. This era is probably the most difficult of all in the history of our race, and I have seen them all!"

This comment made Elu pause and think. Then he said: "Adeevan, you do not appear even as old as me, but I believe you when you say you have seen them all. Tell me, where are you from? You must have quite a story to tell."

"Yes, it would be quite a story, although some of it you already know."

"I do?"

"Yes, but it would be a very long story, too. Too much to tell, I'm afraid."

Elu thought about that for a moment. He realized that Adeevan seemed to be in a mood to talk more than he had been before, so he pressed on, a bit more gently.

"So, please, Adeevan, sit for a while. Tell me your story."

"I wouldn't know where to start, and I'm afraid it would bore you."

Then, in a slightly more intimate way, Elu found the right question: "Adeevan, what are you searching for? I know you are seeking something, what is it?"

To Elu's amazement, this caused quite a reaction from his guest. Adeevan began with a bit of a husky voice, a bit choked up, and had a small tear in one eye.

"It is not a "what", elder, but a "who"…I seek my wife, my dear one, my Khava. I lost her, you see, and I spend all my energy seeking her."

"What happened? How did you lose her?"

It took Adeevan a minute or two to continue. Then he laid

out the story.

"We were very happy, just the two of us. We lived together in a marvelous country. We had all we wanted. We had each other and it was a splendid life. It was like a huge garden. But, then, we were forced to leave our home. Life became harder. We raised a family, and it was good, but we longed to return to our homeland. Then, I lost her, I lost them all, because of my own pride and arrogance…"

Adeevan had to pause for a bit, to gather himself. It was clearly a very emotional story for him to tell, and Elu simply waited for him.

"I tried," he continued, "to return to our former land. I actually found the way. I was back! But, when I tried to find Khava again, I couldn't. She was nowhere I looked. I am still looking, Elu, I am still looking…"

Adeevan broke down for a moment. He had never addressed Elu by his given name, and the bishop realized this was another clue, that the story was still very raw for him.

"Adeevan, tell me about Khava. That's an unusual name. What language is it?"

"Khava was wonderful, Elu. It was as if she was part of me! Her name is from an ancient tongue that you would not know. The name means "life" and she was my life!"

Elu thought for a moment, then something clicked.

"Khava, life…tell me, Adeevan, is there a form of that name in my language?"

"Yes, Elu, there is…um…"Eve", I believe you would say."

"Eve…and "Adeevan"…does it come from the same language?"

"Yes," Adeevan chuckled a bit, "but that is not my name."

"What do you mean it's not your name?"

"It is a title, my friend. Adeevan Zeman in that ancient tongue means "time lord". It is a title given me many, many years ago. My name…well…Khava called me Hadamah."

"Hadamah…that sounds actually familiar."

"Yes, I think it is close to what you would say…probably…"Adam"."

Suddenly, Elu became more alert to the details of Adeevan's story. In fact, his heart began to race. He even had to hold his hands on his chest to steady it.

"Khava and Hadamah, or, Eve and…Adam…and you lived…in a garden?"

Adeevan, or Hadamah, smiled at his friend.

"Now, you remember the story! As I said, you knew the story all along, I simply had to remind you of it."

Elu had to take a few moments to recover from this, but then decided he needed more information.

"So, Hadamah…may I call you that?"

Hadamah nodded.

"So, Hadamah, tell me a bit more about how this happened, how you lost your way."

"In the garden, Elu, things were much simpler. We had none of the complications of this age. We only had each other, the garden, and our Father, who would visit us. There were no "time streams" or any "universe" as you know it. It was simply, I suppose you would say, "linear time"."

"It was just the two of you, in a garden?" asked Elu, in a rather stunned voice.

"Well, there were many animals, but no other "people", at least none like us."

"What do you mean, "like us", exactly?"

"That's probably more information than you want, my

friend," Hadamah said with a bit of a smile."

"So, what happened?" asked Elu.

"Well, we disobeyed, and were forced to leave. It was... how do I say this?...it was cataclysmic! The garden "exploded" in a way and from that explosion, multiple time streams erupted. Each of them led away from our garden and each had their own "space". We were...well, injected, into one of the time streams in sort of a random location, at some distance from its start. This story is also something you have heard, but in different pieces and from different sources. Some of your scientists have theorized about the existence of multiple dimensions to this universe. I think one even guessed the correct number of them! They all arose from this big "bang" when our garden exploded."

Elu was reeling. He was hearing the story of creation, a blended story, bringing together the multiple strands that had somehow survived into the consciousness of his own age. And, he was hearing it from an eyewitness! Finally, he regained his footing and asked another question.

"And you, and Khava, lived then in the time stream?"

"Yes, we lived, we raised a family, but I, in my arrogance, longed to return to our simple life in the garden. I learned how to control time, as you have, and then I found a way to jump from one time stream to another. I was right, I did find one that went "backwards", as you might say. I found the garden, Elu! I was back! But, of course, I needed to get Khava and bring her back. That was the problem. As I tried, the time streams became even more confused, and more interwoven. I have not yet been able to find my way back. That is what I seek. That is why I need "signposts" along the way, such as you have provided me here."

Elu and Hadamah sat in silence for a long while after that. Elu was pretty certain that Hadamah had never told anyone this story before. Then, as they sat there, something else came into Elu's mind.

"Hadamah, my friend, I have someone you need to meet. I suspect, of course, that you know Him, but it has been too long that you have been apart."

"I cannot do that, Elu. I must continue my seeking...He would end my search...I cannot..." Hadamah knew what Elu was proposing, and it scared him terribly.

"Of course, you can, Hadamah. And I will be there with you, to support you. We will find a way. It can be the successful conclusion of your journey. Surely, you are tired of traveling through time and searching and not finding anything."

Hadamah said nothing, but simply sat there, an occasional tear showing up on his cheek.

"You have been there, you have encountered Him in intra-time, haven't you, Elu?"

"Yes, I have. And, yet, here I am."

"I told you not to try it."

"I know. But, come with me, now, to meet Him."

Hadamah slowly got to his feet, and Elu took his arm. They walked out of the bishop's dwelling, across the upper level, and into the cathedral. As they entered, from the front door, instead of the sacristy, they paused. Hadamah hesitated. He stared straight ahead. Elu had been watching his friend, but then turned and looked down the aisle. What he saw astounded him.

In the sanctuary, behind the altar, in the vicinity of the tabernacle, there was an intense glowing light. It seemed to be moving, flowing, and coming at them, but staying in its place at the same time. Neither of them could resist its call. They started down the aisle. Soon they were standing before the altar. The glow intensified, and then they heard the Voice.

"Come to me, for you are heavily burdened. I have longed for you to return, Hadamah!"

They walked around the altar, and stood before the tabernacle. Suddenly, the scene changed. They were back where Elu had stood that other time, when he was alone before the tabernacle. There was the Man on the Cross, before them.

"No!" Yelled Hadamah. "I cannot look! I put you there!"

"No," answered the Man. "I put myself here, Hadamah. I did it for you, but I took it on myself, no one put me here."

There was silence for a bit. Elu stepped back a few steps, to allow Hadamah and the Lord to have their private moment.

"Hadamah," said the Man on the Cross, "Khava is with me and my Father. She longs for you to return. My Father and I long for you to return. Come, our new garden is ready for you. All is forgiven!"

Hadamah raised his head, and looked his Lord directly in the face. He glanced back at Elu with a nod of thanks, then turned and walked directly into the cross! Both he and the Lord, and the Cross itself, suddenly vanished.

Elu stood there for a moment, unsure of what exactly had just happened. Then, he heard the Voice again.

"My good and faithful servant, you, Elu, have done well. Now you must continue to minister to my people. You will guide them back to me. Go, and teach them what you have learned!"

Elu turned and left, to begin this new phase of his life and work.

Epilogue

"Well, Leo, she's looking quite nice, I'd say!"

Elu and Leo were standing on the sidewalk in front of the nearly completely rebuilt Holy Name Cathedral. It had been a difficult time, but with the help of everyone in the tunnels and on the surface, the work had actually gone rather quickly. They had all the rubbish around on the streets of old Chicago to use, of course. It turned out there were quite a few folks with special skills, which helped. All in all, the work had taken only about a year and a half, after about six months of planning.

"Will it be ready in time, bishop, do you think?" Leo asked.

"I'm sure it will be, my friend. We are on track, I believe. We'll have the dedication ceremony next weekend, and the first Mass. Even if we have to reschedule that for the following week, we'll still be in great shape to be ready for the Easter sacraments! Are you getting excited, yet, Brother Leo?"

Leo grinned, and thought for a moment.

"Bishop, it's been my lifelong dream to receive the sacraments, you know that. But, I'm more excited about the others! We are receiving nearly the entire population of the former factions into the church! That is a great thing. You remember the scripture, bishop, I don't need to remind you, but the angels will rejoice more over them than over me!"

Elu chuckled.

"Yes, Leo, you're right, of course."

Just then, Matilda arrived.

"Ah, and here is our chief catechist. What's the lesson this evening, my dear?" asked Elu.

"Tonight, we hear what everyone has chosen for their confirmation names, and my assistant will tell the story of why he chose "Leo" for his name when he joined the friary," Mattie explained.

"That's great! Well, I better get out of your way and let the important work begin."

Elu sauntered on down the street, back to the tunnels, as Mattie and Leo discussed the evenings session. This was going to be the first time they had been able to actually meet inside. The building was finished enough to allow that, so they didn't have to meet on the sidewalk outside anymore. Soon, the folks began arriving. It was essentially all the adults from the two former enemy groups, minus the holdouts. It had been a good process, giving them all a chance to get to know each other, and to reconcile after so many generations of bad feelings. The sessions on forgiveness had been especially poignant, and there hadn't been a dry eye in the entire crowd for several weeks.

Because there were so many to be initiated, Elu and Leo, at Matilda's suggestion, had begun baptizing the children and some of the adults a few weeks ago. They did dozens at each weekend assembly. There were a few families who were planned especially for the Easter service, including Jackie Robinson and her children, Churchy and Maureen and their family, and Chikae, Diondre and their kids. There were still those few missing. Jim Crow and Dikembe were both still fighting each other. They had moved out of the immediate area, and were further south, with just an extra man or two on each side. With a lack of explosives, however, the area was now very quiet. No one went down that way, though, figuring it was simply too dangerous.

Finally, Easter arrived. A huge celebration was planned for the Easter Vigil service, on Saturday evening. Elu vested in his best episcopal robes, in the tunnel sacristy, and then processed up the street all the way to the new Cathedral. He was accompanied by Leo and Matilda and those who were to receive the sacraments that evening. They blessed and lit the new Easter Candle at the entrance to the tunnels and it led all the way uptown.

The Catholic Easter Vigil Service had not been changed since Archbishop Murphy led the escape into the tunnels. Elu had options, of course, but being pretty sentimental, he insisted on having the long version, with all the scripture readings. He also planned on a rather long sermon.

It was an hour into the three-hour service when the Gospel was finally proclaimed, and Elu got out his sermon notes, to begin. He said a few words, but then emotions got the better of him. He choked up, and had to blow his nose a couple times. He started again, but it was no use. He just couldn't continue. That's when he decided to walk down the steps to be closer to his people.

"Brothers and sisters," he began, "I have written a long sermon. I think it's actually pretty good, as sermons go. But, look around you. The best sermon, better than any I could make up, is all around you. It's YOU! YOU, all of you, you are the living and breathing Body of Christ, the Word of God Himself! God's Word is not always verbal. It has been shown in your actions and your love for one another and your reconciliation. I think it's time for sacraments, time for the Holy Spirit to do her work, so, let's get on with it!"

With that, he invited those to receive the sacraments to come forward. It was a blessed time, and Elu had to stop several times to get hold of himself and blow his nose, again, during it all.

The last one to be confirmed was Brother Leo. He had asked to be last. He felt it was more important for the rest of them to approach the altar before him. That caused his reception of the sacrament to be the crowning point of the ceremony, which was not what he was intending, of course, but everyone else considered it to be fitting. After all, after Elu, Leo was the main driver of the whole thing. He was the one who had forged relationships over several years, that made the whole thing work, once the bishop came onto the scene.

After that night, the entire congregation set about slowly rebuilding the city. Elu ordained several men to serve as priests after him. Leo was to be one of them, but in his humility, he declined the honor. However, he remained, of course, the beloved elder until he finally passed away many years later. It was because of all he did for the people that the Cathedral today is named the Cathedral of St. Leo the Friar, with a special meeting place in the basement known as the Bishop Elu Willussit Conference Center.

List of Characters, in approximate order of appearance

Tunnel people
    Bishop Elu (Eli) Wilussit (actually all one name, but used as two)
        Eluwilussit means holy one
        Elu means full of grace
    Matilda (Mattie) Wilussit, Bishop's wife
    Matthew (Matty) Wilussit, Bishop's grandson
    Rachel (Elu and Matilda's daughter) and Tommy, Matthew's deceased parents:
    Miss Theresa, teacher in the tunnels
    Miss Jodie, farmer
    Richard LH, called simply LH, water engineer
    Jennie LH, Richard's wife, called JLH at times
    Darius, a child in the tunnels
    Annie, a child in the tunnels
    Archbishop Tom Murphy, the last surface Archbishop of Chicago, who
        led the escape to the tunnels
    Jennilu, a frequent critic of Elu

Others:
    Brother Leo Mizzl, OSF, the friar who met Elu on the bridge
    Hadamah, the "Adeevan Zeman" (title means "Time Lord")
    Khava, Hadamah's lost wife

White Power Brigade – everyone's last name is Robinson
    Jim Crow Robinson (JCR), leader
    Jackie Robinson, JCR's wife
    JCR and Jackie's children: Tommy (boy) 8 and Leah (girl) 7
    Churchy, 2nd in command
    Maureen, Churchy's wife

Black Power Brotherhood – no one has a last name
    Chikae (name means God's power), leader
    Deiondre, Chikae's wife
    Chikae and Deiondre's children: Kentay (boy) 12 and Kanesha (girl) 10
    Dikembe, 2nd in command
    Kofi, scout and lookout
    Keontae, Deiondre's brother and lookout

www.ingramcontent.com/pod-product-compliance
Lightning Source LLC
Chambersburg PA
CBHW061519120726
48001CB00004B/1361